SAFE CORNERS

A NOVEL

JANE PAILAS-KIMBALL

Healing from the Heart Publishing

Safe Corners

HEALING FROM THE HEART PUBLISHING

ISBN 978-1502432384

First Edition 2014

This edition was prepared for printing by
The Editorial Department
7650 E. Broadway, #308
Tucson, Arizona 85710
www.editorialdepartment.com

Cover image © Trudy Wilkerson

for my husband Paul, lover and friend—

when I had no wings to fly, you flew to me . . .
when there was no dream of mine, you dreamed of me

"In the little world in which children have their existence whosoever brings them up, there is nothing so finely perceived and so finely felt, as injustice. It may be only small injustice that the child can be exposed to; but the child is small, and its world is small . . ."

– Charles Dickens, *Great Expectations*

CHAPTER 1

The oaks and maples shrugged stormy shoulders around the house. The grassy hill drooped into the road. The windows dripped curtains of tears.

Inside, Christina lay on the couch, sorrow soaking her mother's lap.

"I hate God. I hate God," she sobbed.

"I know. I know." Ellen Ladd smoothed her hand down the back of her daughter's sweater whispering, "Let it out. Let it all out. That's my girl."

"Remember, the Lord never gives you more than you can bear," Robert Ladd added, ministerial collar stiff and white at his neck. He sat nearby, bent over, elbows on his knees, head in his hands, a Bible in the center of his lap, his faith resolute.

Brad exploded in fury, "Shit! Shit! Shit!" His fists

pounded the air. An anguished sob flew from his mouth, "Stop the God crap. There's no one out there." Then he tipped straight up the last of the Scotch and fell into one of the loungers.

"I can't live without him. *Won't* live without him." Christina pushed herself up from her mother's lap and rocked back and forth, pulling chunks of hair from both sides of her head into an ache. The pain felt good. "I want to die, to be with him," she choked.

Ellen shushed her daughter back down into her lap and ran her fingers through her thick red curls. "Hush, sweet child. I'm right here. Right here. We'll get through this together."

Together curdled in Christina's throat. There was no together. She was in this alone. Alone without Sammy. Alone in hell.

Later. Alone. In the bathroom. She ran her finger along the edge of a razor and a drop of blood oozed onto the floor. I'll gouge it up and down my wrist, not across it—make sure the blood pumps right out of my body. Then I'll be with him.

She sat on the edge of the toilet seat and watched more drops fall. *Thou shall not kill* trumpeted through her head. How can I do it to Mother? Then she would have lost two of us. And Father would be so ashamed.

Her father's words filled her as from a well with

poisoned water. Throughout her childhood, shooting a stern finger out at her, he'd preached, 'Life isn't *f*air, *e*asy, or *e*qual, Christina. But, whatever life brings, you must always keep faith and trust the Lord.'

Shit. Obviously my life hasn't been *f*air or *e*asy being born to him, having to listen to him wax on about his theory of FEE. And it definitely hasn't been *e*qual. Even when Rusty Bergerman had chanted 'Stick, Stick, Stick,' at my flat thirteen year old body I hadn't been allowed my anger like any normal person. Instead, I'd been punished for bloodying his nose and sent to my room to think about how a pastor's daughter ought to behave.

She jammed the razor next to her jars of Nivea and Cetaphil in the medicine cabinet, wiped up the drops and washed her hands. Then went back to bed. It's dispiriting to accept the way Father is, she thought, but even I have to admit he sincerely believes he's given me the best he has.

Fretfully she flipped over the three by five double-frame lying face down on her nightstand—pictures of Jesus knocking at the door and Jesus with the children at His feet. Why she still kept it there she couldn't say. Maybe it's because Mother gave it to me when I was a little girl, she thought. And sometimes, looking at the face of Jesus, I can feel God's presence.

Idiot! God/Jesus—how can I make sense of all of that? You curse God and then ask Jesus to help you. She threw the frame to the floor, satisfied to hear the glass crack. Father would say Sammy's now one of the children sitting at the Lord's feet. But that's not where he's supposed to be. She went back to the bathroom, grabbed the razor, poised it over her wrist and nipped. But she still couldn't slice and was left with despair crawling through her belly.

For months she wandered around numb, robotic with no direction—legs shaky, buckling as she stumbled into a chair, her mind useless as a wet napkin. Her normally shiny hair hung greasy around her shoulders and she didn't care. Her slim tall body barely hung together and she didn't notice. Lucky Brad, she'd think. He can go back to work—something I can't do. How could I work with other people's children when the child who's been my reason for being is gone?

Worst was that while her grief splashed all over their world, Brad's had become secreted in a dark cavern she wasn't allowed to enter. After that first night his face had become buttoned over—a blank pallet, stony, stoic, silent. He seemed to have completely detached himself from her. And he would never—ever—talk about Sammy. Even on the nights when her nightmares left her wailing, he'd rub her shoulders, kiss her arm, but wouldn't say a word. Not one about their lost child.

Her pain spread between them. Why won't he talk to me, she brooded. Shows how much God's deserted us—allowing us to become divided when we should be leaning into each other. Whoever said you'll find God in the abyss is wrong. Dead wrong.

Gradually rage flooded over the numbness, fury racing through her, carnivorous, ready to chew up anyone on her scope. No one was spared. The UPS gal at the front door. A neighbor soliciting for some children's fund—she should've known better. But Christina evened the score by slamming the door in their pale faces. She didn't give a shit about other people's children or about any gift package even if it came straight from the White House.

And most enraging was her local pastor. "I'm sure God has a plan for you in all of this," he said, patting her arm as she slouched on the couch, tears streaming down her face. "You need to trust Him."

Christina had never liked him and now his smoothed down hair and smoothed over face infuriated her. She jumped up. "Please. I need to be left alone. I doubt I'll ever trust God again—if He's even there behind the curtain."

"Now Christina . . ."

Without a word she crossed the room, motioned to the door and, as he left, blew a spit at his back.

Even her best bud Sarah got it. When Sarah stopped

over, her golden caramel-colored face drawn with concern, her hair in corn rows with bright beads, Christina screamed, "Leave me alone! Stop calling morning, noon, and night! Stop dropping by!" Just the thought of Sarah's two beautiful daughters, Allene and Allison, safely tucked in each night seared her with jealousy. And right there, with her friend watching, she threw Sarah's freshly backed zucchini bread on the floor and stomped on it.

It was a hard healing.

Not soothed when Brad came in one evening around the ten month anniversary of Sammy's death saying, "We should take a cruise."

"A cruise?" Christina swallowed hard and stared at him. "How's that going to help when we're so uncomfortable with each other? When you won't talk to me?"

"Come on, Christina, give it a try."

So she picked up some brochures.

"These on the Greek Isles look good," Brad said. "Or, how 'bout these to Scandinavia?"

"They're all so far away."

"Of course they're far away. That's the point. What do you mean?"

"Far away from Sammy." Christina closed her eyes and shook her head.

"Tina, don't be ridiculous."

"I just can't go away. I need to be here near him."

"Tina, please. Sam's not here."

"I know, but . . . well, I might as well say it. We're no longer working. Without Sammy we're a comb without teeth."

"Tina, please. We lost Sammy, a tooth in the comb. We haven't lost the whole comb. *We're* the comb—you and I."

Christina jumped up from the table and stood next to her husband, arms spread out, palms up, hands bouncing. "Then why won't you talk to me about what happened to Sammy? Why do you work longer and longer hours? Do you know how that makes me feel?"

Brad stared at her, silent, jaw muscles twitching.

"Like a reject—totally sick inside. That's how I feel. I can't see how going on a cruise will help us."

"Damn you and the comb. Sammy was a helluva lot more than a tooth! I miss him every day—can't fucking believe he'll never come jumping into our bed each morning. But he's *gone.*"

"Then let's stack our grief together. Comfort each other. Talk about what we've lost."

"Christina, I just can't. So that's that." Anger shot up filling his face, busying his Adam's apple. He curled his fingers into his palm and knuckled the edge of the top brochure. Then he threw the pile on the floor, dumped his coffee into the sink and left, slamming the side door without another word.

Christina felt relieved. Good. I can't stand his face, she thought. I can't stand him, period. But, minutes later, panic filled her. What have I done? Was I too stubborn about the cruise? Too insistent that we talk about Sammy? Have I messed up a chance for us to find a way back to each other?

No! If he won't talk to me about what's happened, I'm done. She picked up the brochures, stuffed them back into the AAA envelope, wiped some lipstick from the rim of her cup and loaded the dishwasher. And for a while enjoyed the warmth of being right.

Until the words her father had often used slipped to the front of her brain. 'Christina,' he'd say, 'just because you're right doesn't mean you're right. The Lord teaches us to be humble.'

The Lord, she sighed, pulling an afghan around her shoulders and folding into her rocker, a pillow pressed into her belly as she thought back with a heavy heart to how fully she'd loved God as a child. To how happy she'd been pushing higher and higher on her swing sing-songing, *How do you like to go up in a swing, up in the air so blue*, feeling she was flying closer to God, her eyes closed as she tried to picture what He looked like.

Was He a bearded old man sitting on a throne or was

He a giant like the one in *Jack and the Beanstalk*? Not even her father could tell her what God looked like. So she'd colored her own picture of Him as a big smiling face puffed up in a golden pink cloud and pasted Him on the fridge, telling her mother he was Sky Guy.

Faith used to be a river than ran through me, she thought. It energized me and filled me with hope. But, when Sammy died, a plug was pulled draining me of that. And without it I feel unanchored—left on a ledge—half wanting to take that old leap but pulled back by a thick cord of doubt. Which I know is a huge turn-off for Brad. While the turn-off for me is his refusal to talk about our lost child. But how can I never talk about Sammy, Christina agonized. Impossible.

He's like an evanescent bubble always floating above my head. And, when I talk about him, I feel that bubble—for a sliver of a moment—slipping down closer to me. Wouldn't any mother who's lost a child feel something like that? Wouldn't any mother do anything to pull the bubble closer? Of course any mother would. She nodded in agreement with herself as she threw the AAA envelope into the recycle bin.

Then she switched gears. But maybe I have to accept that Brad can only deal with his grief through denial. So, while I'm right, I may not *be* right. I'll give him a call.

No answer. Damn him, he won't pick up. Christina began to feel panicky. She *had* screwed up. As much as she'd been relieved when he left, she now wanted him back. She gulped water, paced back and forth, dialed again and again, finally dragged herself into the shower. Then flopped on the bed and bawled, agitating away any hope for a restful sleep.

Okay, she thought the next morning as she pulled on her navy sweats. I'm actually losing my mind. Ever since Sam I can't keep a grip. I think I'm better and then I'm not. Looking listlessly around her normally neat bedroom, a mess with last night's clothes flung all over, she rubbed her dry heels with A & D, slipped on some woolen socks and began to pick up.

Began and then fell back on the bed. How can I keep a grip when I watched my own child getting run over? *When I was responsible for his getting run over?*

There. I've said it. Said it for the hundredth time—maybe the millionth—mostly to myself, but more times than I can count to both Mother and Sarah. Brad of course will never listen. He must think if he listens to me he'll feel obliged to say I forgive you. And I know I can never expect that.

I can't expect that from him when I'll never be able to forgive myself. How, on that morning, I'd hurried through the gate to the mailbox, picked through the

advertisements 'til I came to the envelope I was looking for and excitedly opened it, absent-mindedly tou-
sling Sammy's blonde curls as he parked his red Radio
Flyer wagon and got on his trike. And seconds later flew
through the gate into the SUV.

I'd been so eager to learn if I'd passed the licensing
exam to practice as a clinical psychologist that I hadn't
carefully closed the gate. Meaning, I killed my own son.
She pulled the blinds shut and curled into the warmth
of her unmade bed. Then brooded away the passing
days with regret, feeling raw, held together with safety
pins, her energy dripping through the gaps like she was
vanishing into the shadows without a way back.

She spent numbing hours watching the insane antics
on the Jerry Springer Show, the oddball suits on Judge
Judy, and incredulous hours watching re-run clips of
President Clinton denying he had sexual relations with
Monica Lewinsky. The world has gone crazy with
me, she thought, lifting her shirt and nipping the skin
around her ribs with the razor she now kept in a side
drawer of her reading stand.

Young girls are right, she nodded, chomping her
teeth together. The cuts hurt like hell and hell feels
good.

On better days she was comforted by paging over and
over through her two photo albums, year one and year

two. She'd insisted on hard copy—pictures she could hold in her hand, mount in a book, pat at, love at, as she put them in order. She tried to assemble year three from the snaps she'd stored in envelopes until there was time, but it was too hard. Looking at one of the last ones of Sammy, smiling on his new trike, waving at her, baby teeth shining, sent her to bed for the day.

Does he know, she wondered, wherever he is, that I would've pulled the rainbow from the sky for him to slide up and down on? That I would've blown bubbles in color for him to jump through? That I would've tickled his nose with daisies until he fell over laughing? Her heart ached thinking of all she now *couldn't* do for him. Well I had my chance, she anguished, and I blew it with the gate. She buried herself into the blankets and tried to blot out that scene by brooding some more about how she'd now chased away Brad.

Does he miss me, she wondered. I can't imagine life without him. But maybe he's already setting up his own apartment. Stop! You're going too far! Ease up! Get a grip! She dropped her head into her hand, elbow on her desk, and inhaled one, two, three, four. Then exhaled one through eight, coaching herself into calmness. She had a lot to think about.

Finally, one evening two weeks later, as she was trying to escape into a new novel, she heard his key in the door. Oh my God! He's back! She tried to slow herself down. Took a few deep breaths. Then jumped up as he stepped around the corner.

"Tia!" She flew into his arms. Kissed his neck murmuring, "I've missed you so much."

"Me too."

"Thank God you're back. I'm sorry about the comb thing. Let's try to get it together."

"I had to come back, Tia. This's been all wrong."

"I know." She cozied her head into his shoulder, happy he was calling her 'Tia', their Sammy word.

"I'll open a bottle of wine. You get the cheese and crackers, and let's watch a Seinfeld re-run,"

"Okay . . . But Hon, don't you think we first should talk—to look at what's been happening between us?"

"No. We need to chill. Come on, I'll get the wine."

It felt out of sync to her but she went along. And, as they settled in on the couch, their socked feet on the coffee table watching their favorite sitcom, she rubbed her foot against his, thinking, this is what happiness is.

When the re-run was over, she shifted slightly on the couch, smiled up at him and asked, "So can we talk now?"

"Come here," he answered, pulling her closer and shifting her body under his, softly caressing her and filling her with Zachary.

CHAPTER 2

Christina loved the emerald green dress she'd splurged on for the big do Brad's company was throwing that evening in Manhattan. She kept smoothing her hand down the front as she turned back and forth in front of the mirror to assure herself her tiny bump didn't show.

Tonight, she nodded to herself, is an important one for Brad. Big brass will be there to party while actually looking over their top sales people, to measure what promise each holds for their software company. I have to be up, she thought, to rise to the occasion and make Brad proud. It's an effort because my feet still feel locked in cement but I want to do it, to be there for him.

She turned from the mirror, took a deep breath, and walked over to the window for a quiet minute to gather herself together. She loved their wide and spacious lawn and remembered how pleased she and Brad had been to find that Sarah and John lived right across the way.

Late on their move-in afternoon Sarah had handed Brad a casserole when he opened the door. 'Hope you're hungry,' she'd said with a wide, welcoming smile.

'Starved,' Christina had answered, grabbing the dish. 'God, this move's almost wasted us.'

'That's the way we felt a year ago,' John had said, 'totally swamped and too tired to go out for food'

'Well, thanks for bringing this over,' Brad replied as the two men shook hands.

'You're more than welcome,' Sarah said looking around at all the boxes. 'But this mess will be gone before you know it. And I'm sure you'll love it here. It's a great neighborhood for children when you're ready. So far we have two girls and we're hoping one day to try for a boy. Although the only thing that really matters is that any baby we have will be healthy'.

'Exactly the way I feel,' Christina had replied. And right then she knew she and Sarah would become great friends.

How happy Brad and I were that day, she reminisced, as we settled into this beautiful colonial outside of Stamford in southern Connecticut. And happier still when, after Sammy came along, we'd installed a black wrought iron gated fence along the bottom of the grassy, gently sloping hill, curving it around the arbor vitae, rhododendron and azalea bushes on either side of the hill. We were so innocent, she thought. If only yesterday had a string attached to it so I could pull it back.

As a child—sometimes after a Sunday service, sometimes playing in the living room at the manse—she'd heard her mother softly consoling one woman or another, 'Give it time and the Lord will heal your hurt'.

Well, she thought, I don't know when or if that can ever happen for me. Especially since I'm no longer sure He's even there.

Then she remembered the afternoon she'd hidden the razor and picked up the matches. What would it feel like to start with the fluffy down comforter, watch the flames catch as she lay in bed frying? Remembering, Christina shuddered. Oh my God, I really was on the brink of insanity.

So maybe God *had* been with her that day, drawing her to Sammy's room, where she slipped down on the floor and caressed his toys, first one then another until, exhausted, she had folded into herself on his bed and sobbed myself to sleep.

Don't go back to that, she cautioned herself. Not tonight. Shake it off. Focus on how much you love this house because it's where Sammy lived. Picture yourself falling into that pile of leaves, breathing in all their color. She closed her eyes and took a deep breath but the gray remained.

"You ready yet?" Brad asked entering the room. "I don't want to be late."

Okay, she thought, tuck away the gray. Do it for Brad. "Me either." She smiled up at him, loving his glorious aqua green eyes and his handsome face with its proud square chin, its dominant nose—a small just-right rise in the middle. "I need you to finish pulling up the zipper on this dress and then I'll be set."

"God, Tia, you look beautiful!"

"I don't show?"

"Not at all." He spun her around in a tight embrace and nuzzled her neck saying, "You're ravishing. Phew! I'd rather zip you out than zip you in."

She flushed with pleasure, playfully flicking her eyelashes and tossing her long hair as she spun around on five inch heels. "Keep that up and we'll never get out of here," Brad laughed. "Come on, let's go."

This feels good, Christina thought, as they hustled out to the car. It's been touch and go since our separation. Sometimes Brad's right there for me and other times he drifts into the aloofness I hate. Sarah thinks I should see a therapist. But I don't know . . .

As they drove down the Saw Mill Parkway Brad's

hand reached for hers. "Look at that bumper sticker—*What if the Hokey-Pokey IS all that it's all about.* Who thinks up these things anyway?"

Christina slid into their comfort zone. "Don't know, but I'm glad you didn't buy vanity plates for my new Camry."

"Because you said you didn't want them. Personally, I thought you'd like to have CF PHD on your car."

"No. I like anonymity."

"Like you're hanging out at a lesbian stripper's club or gambling all day at the casino in Ledyard and don't want to be caught."

"That's not the point. After years of being a pastor's kid, feeling like a bug under a microscope, I like my privacy." Christina shifted in her seat. "But here's a bumper sticker I saw the other day which made me think—*No Jesus. No Peace. Know Jesus. Know Peace.*"

"Oh God, you're going there again?" He shook his head, let go of her hand.

"Yeah. Made me think of *Footprints*, that beautiful embroidery hanging in Mother's kitchen. Remember it? The seeker asked the Lord why sometimes there were two sets of footprints in the sand and at other times only one. 'The times when you saw only one set, my child, were when I was carrying you,' the Lord said."

Brad shook his head. "I guess you can take the girl

out of the manse but you can't take the teachings of the manse out of the girl."

"All I can say is that on days when I laid curled up in bed cursing God, I'd picture the face of Jesus and somehow feel comforted. So maybe, despite my doubts, the Lord did carry me along."

"If it helps you to think that, go ahead. Just don't talk to me about it. And I can tell you if I'd seen that sticker I would've felt offended. It's pushing someone else's religious belief right into my face. And I resent that. But then, I've never understood the God/Jesus connection. For me it's a crock."

Christina started to bristle then stopped herself thinking, I don't quite get it myself. Although, she modified, seeing Jesus in a picture makes God seem more real—just as when I see Grandma's picture she seems alive and immediate to me. But, oh boy, I better back off. She placed her hand on Brad's thigh. "I'm so thankful we're having this baby, aren't you?"

"Of course. It'll be good for both of us."

"But let's not forget Sammy."

"Tina, don't go there, please."

"But I can't help thinking about him. Why won't you ever talk about him?"

"It's best if we leave all of that alone."

Christina bit her bottom lip. I don't get how he can split off like that—not even wanting to remember the cute things—like the way Sammy crawled into his lap coaxing for a puppy while licking Brad's cheek. I'd cracked up over that. Or how can he not remember the way Sammy had waved his cereal bowl at us one morning squealing, 'See Tia, awl gone.' Well, she thought, I guess a mother treasures memories like that in a way that's different from fathers.

But somehow that didn't fit. Brad had been such a loving, present father. There's something I can't grab hold of, she thought. Something that's keeping him all bottled up. She closed her eyes, picturing Sammy on his little trike. I wonder if that's it. Sam was killed riding his bike and I wonder if Brad won't talk about him because he was the one to insist on buying the red trike. That's a stretch, she thought, but could be.

On their trip to Ogunquit Sammy's last summer they'd spent their days lazying on low slung chairs on the soft white sand, their heads propped as they read and watched Sammy sifting sand into one pail, then pouring it into another. And, when he tired of that, one of them helped him fill the pails with water to build a sand castle or took him into the shallow waves swinging him around as he squealed in delight—a family time— unlike the days on their honeymoon ten years earlier when she and Brad had had secret sex in the waves oblivious to the fifty-eight degree water.

On their last evening in Maine, Christina

remembered, Sammy had almost knocked the snack bag out of her arms as he dragged her through the open door of the hardware store and climbed onto the small red tricycle. She hadn't been sure he was ready for it but Brad nodded yes as they watched Sammy pedaling down the aisle. 'He's already a little jock,' Brad joked, his face crinkling with pleasure around his sunburn. 'So I say we buy it.' And that had been that.

Christina sighed remembering how, when they got back to their motel, all Sammy wanted to do was ride his trike around and around the parking lot until finally Brad picked him up and carried him in, hugging him close as the child wailed away. You never know which moments are the precious ones, she thought. Maybe that's where Brad's stuck—at that red bike.

But I can't go there right now. I have to shut up or he'll *really* get pissed. And I don't want to ruin his big evening.

Brad must've sensed her mood for he reached over and stroked her hand pressing it again into his thigh. Gratefully Christina lifted his hand and kissed it thinking, tonight he's mine and I'm his.

"I'll be interested in what you think of some of the guys you'll be meeting, especially Ray," Brad said. "He's probably my biggest competitor for promotion to head of New England sales. And I have to hand it to you—you *do* have a way of seeing what's beneath the surface in people. That's why you're such a cool and excellent psychologist."

Christina grinned as his compliment oozed in. "Yeah. As a kid I learned a lot about the shadow side of people. I don't think Mother ever realized how much I took in playing behind the piano at the far end of our living room as she counseled God knows how many parishioners. That was her forte. Faith was Father's. It was what his congregation wanted from him. But they brought their sorrows to Mother."

"Anyway, this guy Ray—he's always super cooperative, willing to help—almost over-the-top that way. Somehow too good to be true. I keep wondering what he has in his back pocket."

"I'll give him a good look."

When they arrived at The Plaza Christina felt excited and asked, "Did you ever read about the misadventures of Eloise, the rich little girl who lived on the top floor of this hotel? I was totally enchanted by her as a child."

"Nope. I was too busy reading about the Hulk and other super heroes."

"I wish I had known you then."

"A scrubby little kid with black and blue knees?"

"Maybe not," she laughed. "And you wouldn't have given twiggy me a second glance."

"But look how happily well-rounded you turned out."

"And soon to be even more rounded out. You ready?"

"Absolutely." He patted her behind before she took his arm and pointed up with her other hand. "Just look how regal it is with its rounded turrets and peaks, the flags of different countries fluttering above Fifth Avenue.

"It *is* old world beauty," Brad agreed. "When I was at Columbia I used to bring girlfriends here for tea in the Palm Court. Impressed the hell out of them. But in 1999 the property's really showing its age."

"True, but I'm psyched to be here. I love the elegance—the marble floors and all the gold leaf in the crystal chandeliers! I know it's almost a hundred years old, but I don't care. I think it's beautiful."

Christina's spirits lifted still more as they walked into the opulent ballroom and Brad's co-workers enthusiastically swarmed around. "This is my wife Christina. She's a psychologist," Brad said, his arm wrapped tightly around her waist.

"We've heard a lot about you." Ray was the first to chime in as he sandwiched Christina's hand. Others shook her hand more casually and slapped Brad on the shoulder while the women gave him pecks on his cheeks, European style.

Christina was both pleased and put off by the way the men eyed her up and down, then swung their eyes in lazy circles checking out every woman in the room, hungry for red meat. Hm-m, she thought, Brad would probably act the same way if I weren't here. Oh well, I guess boys will be boys.

Brad proudly made a real effort to draw her into the conversation of each little group. And she hung on to the conversation as much as possible, but when the talk got to intense almost wild speculations about what lay ahead with computers—utilization of the entire software ecosystem linking all digital media, almost incomprehensible jargon about 64-bit computing and multi-core architecture—she felt her eyes beginning to channel into her eyebrows.

She squeezed Brad's hand and drifted over to pick up another white wine and people-watch with the small crowd around the plush bar decked out with fuchsia and purple orchids and an array of exotic looking delicacies. She stabbed a king-size mushroom stuffed with crab-meat and gazed around at the women.

This's what I always do, she thought—zoom in on the other women. I guess I'm always comparing myself, anxious about how I look, how I measure up. Must be a left-over from my twiggy stick days. Doesn't matter if it's the Macy's Clinque girl with her firm round calves and narrow contoured ankles below her perky dress and white jacket, or the hourglass bartender at this party with her 44Ds. God, what would it be like to sport melons like those? She gawked, then forced her eyes away. But not before noticing all the men around the bar also gawking, probably wondering, she thought, what it would be like to hold those babies in their hands.

Well I can't blame them, she mused. I have a kaboom fantasy life of my own imagining running my hands over a differently muscled chest, feeling the thrill of someone new entering me. Not that I'd act on it, she told herself, snapping out of her reverie to re-focus on the other women at the party.

Not the wives, but Ted's co-workers, were almost uniformly dressed in swishy black silk pants or sleek black designer jeans with alluring low-cut blouses, or in stylish black dresses cut above their knees highlighting toned legs slipped into five and six inch heels. The only one who jumped out as different was a gorgeous blonde Christina scrupulously scanned wondering how frequently she worked with Brad.

The woman was breath-taking—had dazzled Christina earlier with her chocolate eyes spangled with gold boring into her own as she'd half whispered, 'We adore Brad. So glad to finally meet you.' Then had floated away, her long creamy hair shimmering in a loose pageboy over the shoulders of her silk steel-gray suit jacket.

Now Christina's stomach pinched as she watched her breezing around the room, touching this one on the shoulder, nodding and smiling at another in what Christina thought was a highly seductive way. She was clearly working the crowd and moving back toward Brad. But Christina got there first, smoothed the sleeve of his jacket and linked her arm in his. When the woman dropped her lips to his ear, leaning so her breast almost touched his arm, Christina pulled him in closer and bit her lip, glad the party was winding down.

On the way home Brad enthused about his friends. As he lowered his window and pointed his elbow outside, he smiled over at Christina. "They're a great bunch and I was very proud of how easily you mixed in with everyone—even with the nerdy ones. Believe me, they're the important guys—the brains who come up with the innovative stuff so that sales people like myself have outstanding products to take to our customers."

"Actually, the evening was more interesting and fun than I expected and I was proud of you too. God, that air feels good."

"So what about Ray?"

"I'd look out for him if I were you. I think under all

that outer charm he has a huge manipulative streak you can't trust."

"I knew you'd do a quick read. What made you see manipulation?"

"Oh God, the way he hovered around me—getting me more wine, complementing me with a sly gleam in his eye. That sort of thing—like I was the president's wife. He was definitely in over-drive and it felt creepy."

"Hm-m. I'll keep that in mind."

Then Christina cautiously dipped a toe into the water. "Tell me more about that stunning blonde."

"Isabelle? What a gal! She works in Manhattan in charge of national and international marketing. She's amazing, don't you think?"

"Don't know. I just met her." She took a deep breath. "Amazing—how?"

"The way she carries herself for one thing. Totally confident, almost cocky. Because she knows how much we value her talent for coming up with creative ways of displaying our products."

"How often does she work in Connecticut?"

"Hardly ever. But I sit in on meetings with her when I'm in the City. She's a true leader—very well liked."

"She struck me as hugely sexy."

"Strikes a lot of people that way. It's part of her M.O. But actually she's all business and one of the persons who can help me advance to head of technological sales. She's very influential in the company—the type of gal I envision aiming to be president of the company some day."

"Just so you don't envision her in your arms."

"Don't go there, Christina. Right now *you're* what I want! Thank God we're home. My balls are aching."

When he swept her off her feet and onto the kitchen floor she melted into him like sizzling butter.

CHAPTER 3

Dead leaves swirled around the parking lot on an overcast brittle November day as, four months pregnant, Christina slumped up to the front door of the therapist's office building. Not really an office building but a large cream-colored house with neatly trimmed bushes bordering the front, gold and scarlet chrysanthemums above in long bronze window boxes.

Physically she felt great thanks to all her bicycling but emotionally she was a wreck. And, as she gave her name to the secretary, she shivered with regret wondering why she had let Sarah talk her into this. I'm just a crazy pregnant woman, she thought. This's a waste of time. I'm the one always telling *others* they need therapy. Now here I am. Oh well . . .

"Dr. Osbourn is ready to see you."

"Thanks." Reluctantly, she followed the young woman to a half-opened polished door where she was greeted by the fiftyish Dr. Osbourn. Most of the shrinks she'd worked with as a school psychologist had been male, distant, and edgy. So she'd been ready for that.

And was pleased to find Dr. Osbourn entirely different. She smiled warmly as she shook Christina's hand and ever so slightly nodded her head as though saying I'm glad you're here.

Tall and slender, Dr. Osbourn wore a silk dress of floating pastel colors with a mandarin collar and nodded Christina toward a straight-backed chair while she settled into a cherry rocker. As she took a few moments to glance over Christina's intake sheet, Christina looked around the office.

The walls were painted a soft blush and Christina immediately noticed that each of the pictures hanging around the room portrayed a mother and child. In one, a woman wearing a blue robe was bending over a crib caressing the cheek of a newborn. In another, a Native American woman held two toddlers, her eyes riveted on the younger of the two. And in a third, a Viking mother was walking across waves of water, an infant in her arms.

On the wall of shelves to the side of the doctor's desk intermingled with books, stood an array of beautiful

Navajo baskets familiar to Christina from the summer she'd backpacked in Arizona. The baskets, like the ones she'd purchased, had been woven in the traditional Navajo colors of red, white and black—the black representing the darkness of night and the clouds which bring rain, the white for the four sacred mountains of Navajo tradition, and the red for the life-giving rays of the sun.

Then, just as Christina was beginning to relax, even smiling as she noticed a huge grinning teddy bear on the floor next to the desk, Dr. Osbourn turned to her asking, "So Christina, what brings you to therapy?"

"I don't really know. A friend suggested I come."

"Why did your friend suggest that?"

"Because she knows I'm unhappy."

"All right. So you *do* know why you're here."

"I guess."

"Take a deep breath, keep both feet flat on the floor, look straight at me and breathe into the words 'I'm here because I'm unhappy'."

Christina blinked down at her clenched hands and began to shake all over, tears rolling down her cheeks. It was a wrenching session. As she left, she felt anxious, worse than when she'd arrived, like she was struggling to balance on a thin wiggly wire. Although her graduate work had included participating both as a client and a

counselor in a variety of counseling training sessions—
Rogerian, cognitive, reality, neurolinquistic—this was
her first go at deep therapy and she didn't yet realize that
gestalt therapy with its focus on here-and-now aware-
ness would take her through a gripping life-changing
process.

But she soon learned. The early weeks were particularly horrendous. Christina thought she would die.
Because Marlene (as Dr. Osbourne asked to be called)
refused, after the initial telling, to let her go over and
over the story of Sammy's death and the increasing
problems in her marriage. "We will get back to all of
that," she said, pushing her glasses up on her nose. "But
first we have a more immediate issue. Christina, I want
you to visualize your unborn baby on that pillow in the
empty chair I've pulled up."

"How can I do that?"

"Let yourself go and visualize the baby as though he
were really there. Talk to him."

"I don't know how to do that. Besides, what's the
point? It's not why I've come to therapy." Marlene said
nothing as Christina wrestled with her stubbornness,
refusing to say one word.

Their second session ended with Marlene saying,
"Your refusal to talk to your new baby is a way you
remain connected to Sammy. Until you talk to your

new baby from a place of realness, no matter how harsh your words, you won't have cleared a place for him in your life and in your heart."

"Sarah," Christina said the next day, "I think this therapist's wacky."

"No Christina. I know her well and she's excellent at seeing between the crevices. Please keep going. Come here." She pulled Christina into a tight hug and whispered, "I'll hold you in my prayers."

She can pray all she wants, Christina thought. I'm not going back. However, that week as her nightmares about Sammy became even darker and scarier, she decided to give it another try.

But again, therapy seemed too hard. She sat in silence as Marlene softly reassured her. "You need to go down into your pain, Christina. That's the only way up. You have so much hurt and anger. So first of all we must deal with your feelings about your new baby. You need to work through those before you can fall in love with him and give him the safe corner he needs."

Marlene paused, "You see, Christina, we all need safe corners—safe corners within ourselves and safe corners in our relationships. You've been shattered by your loss and have lost your sense of safety. So we have a lot of work to do."

Christina thought yah dah, yah dah and kept her

hands clenched in fists. I can't do it. I can't do it, went round and round in her head. The minutes ticked away. Frustrated, she looked at her watch thinking, why am I paying good money just to sit here? God damn! She wants me to talk to that damn pillow I will.

She reached for the pillow.

"Picture your new baby, Christina, and talk to him."

Christina felt incensed that she'd gotten herself into this spot. She edged her fingers along the sides of the pillow pinching it until finally her anger pushed her forward and she poked a finger into the pillow. "Why couldn't you have been a girl? Don't you know you can never replace Sammy? Don't you know you'll never be able to trust me? I'm a terrible mother." On and on. It was a death-like purge.

Especially the part about blaming the baby because he wasn't a girl. She had an excruciating time with that. Because, after she'd first learned she was pregnant, she'd immediately begun drawing pictures in her head about how much fun it would be to shop for cute frilly pink dresses, to pin bows in her daughter's hair, to polish her tiny nails, to take her to ballet. Just thinking about all of that filled her with joy and she named her baby Laurel Rose.

She even got into the habit of watching mothers with their little girls. One day, having a tea latte in the mall, she felt her heart pounding as she watched a bright-faced twentyish mother smoothing the hair of her daughter. The child, in her Winnie-the-Pooh blouse, was sitting in a stroller stretching her tiny neck so that, as she reached for the taco chips, her chin met the table. What an adorable Hershey-kiss face, Christina thought. I can't wait for Laurel Rose.

Then she'd learned she was carrying another boy. What a blow. Again and again she cried Why God and slid the razor, slicing a deep gash under her sweater. Why couldn't You let me have Laurel Rose? Am I such a bad person that You have to continually beat up on me like you did with the Jews wandering in the wilderness? Haven't I been through enough? But then, actually, *You aren't there*. So why should I keep talking to You?

For session-after-session Christina was in agony. But, as she gained confidence in Marlene, she was able to go deeper and deeper, emptying out her anger and resistance.

Then slowly, miraculously, magic! As she felt the soft pitter-pat of her baby, Christina came alive with love for her son and agreed with Brad about naming him Zachary.

At last, when Marlene asked her to talk to him in the empty chair she reached over and cuddled the pillow saying, "I love you, little Zachary. And guess what? I bought you a beautiful new crib and painted your room blue with a teddy bear border." Her bonding with her new son had become deep and immutable.

But, although Brad shared her joy about the pregnancy, he was slipping away again, unable it seemed to maintain the closeness and passion they'd shared the night of the party. It's as though since Sammy, Christina thought, the magnet connecting us has lost its force. But it sure pulled us together with a POW when we met that eighties summer on our way to a Rainbow Family of Living Lights gathering.

Her thirty-five pound backpack jammed with sleeping bag, tent, toilet paper, eating utensils, biodegradable soap and other essentials had shifted sending her off balance as she hiked down the steep trail. That's when Brad had reached over and braced her elbow.

"Thanks," she'd whispered, hating the give-away flush she felt filling her face and neck.

But everything after that had come easily as together they snaked their way down the dusty path edged with aspens and brilliant wild flowers into the desert canyon.

They agreed that coming to this counter-culture hippie gathering which originated in 1972 and regrouped annually the first week of July in a national forest felt freeing, completely removing them from the mainstream lives they'd both chosen.

"Only when I'm using the open latrine do I wonder why I keep coming back," Christina remembered Brad saying.

"For me," she'd replied, "coming to Rainbow helps me keep my priorities straight. Not that I agree with all the issues Rainbows are into."

"Yeah. I'm all for peace and a green environment, not so much for legalization of marijuana."

"Really? That surprises me. I think legalization would be smart. It'd bring in a lot of tax money for one thing."

"Good point. I don't know . . . But—what the hell—maybe I should rethink it." And as Brad pressed his hand into the small of her back a rush of excitement had fired through her. Christina sighed remembering.

Their connection had been magical and hot. As they reached the valley, they'd been swept into the whirl of tie-dye shirts, fringed jeans and vests, diaphanous dresses and, after setting up tents, had jumped naked without a second thought into the freezing river. Then had fallen into each other's arms in a sea of desire on the inch thick mat in her tent—totally, sensually blissed out by the calm flowing from the piping flutes and softly strumming guitars.

God, what joy, she thought. Brad hadn't been her first lover, but he was one of her best. "Show me your wild side, Christina," he'd whispered. "Do you like how this feels? Oo, when you touch me there I love it. That's it. Just let yourself go." She'd flown.

But now she *wasn't* flying and tears drenched her lashes. She'd splurged on a lacy black satin nightgown and a red silk teddy, but the sparkle never happened.

It's all my fault, she mourned. There's too much unsaid about the child we've lost—about how he died. I hope that things will change when Zachary arrives.

CHAPTER 4

Slowly Christina began to heal. Time, she thought, has made up its mind that I should move out of the darkness. That I should take hold of the good in my life and move on—do what I never thought I could do—live without Sammy.

She knew the picture of him lying in the street would never leave her but she'd grown tired of glooming around. Tired of sobbing in Sammy's room fondling his toys. Tired of begging Brad to talk. Tired of wondering how Job with his lost sons and daughters, his loathsome sores, had maintained faith.

But most of all, she began to feel renewed because now Zachary was humming within her. When Sammy died, she thought, my sorrow piled up the way snow does during a winter storm. And there wasn't a plow on earth mighty enough to shovel it away. Until now, tiny Zachary, warm in my womb, is doing the job.

It's as though, she thought, thanks to Zachary and my therapy with Marlene, all of me—body, mind, and spirit—has joined hands carefully knitting over and around my wound. Today I woke up with the words of my favorite poem rolling through my head: *I am the master of my fate. I am captain of my soul.*

And that's the damn truth, she thought, as she headed for the shower. Time I remember I *am* master of my fate, captain of my soul.

But no! I *wasn't* master of my fate when Sam died. She slapped her forehead. Shut up, please! Stop going back angsting over and over about what happened. Angsting about God. Because who knows?

Was it God Himself Who had been master of my fate that day? Grumpy in heaven, inhaling through some cosmic straw and sucking Sammy away from me? Or had He been up there crying for me? Or maybe not up there at all?

Whatever, she sighed, drying herself and slipping into her clothes. All I know is that I have to pick myself up and at least become captain of my soul. She went downstairs, lighter inside, phoned the Fellow Travelers Soup Kitchen, and signed on to serve breakfast three mornings a week.

Then, newly energized, she dug through her miscel-laneous drawer for the hooks she needed to hang her new picture. She lifted the heavy frame, shifting its weight from side-to-side, estimating how high it should go.

She loved the richness of the lush scarlet peonies in the tall cut-glass vase overlooking a bowl filled with oranges, pinkish green pears, and speckled bananas. She knew it wasn't too original but she liked it because it said warm home, a home where little boys would like to live. A home hopefully without the contradictions of the home she grew up in.

I give Mother all the credit in the world for trying to keep things soft, she thought, but Father was tough, hard for me to fathom. Sometimes I feel at such odds within myself that I just want to run away and pretend I'm some-one else—someone with true inner peace. As if running away would give me that. She frowned as she centered the picture on the wall on one side of the kitchen table.

A few weeks later after Christina and Sarah had finished paging through fabric samples for a valence in Sarah's downstairs bath, Christina paused and nudged her shoulder into Sarah's. They were sitting next to each other on a window seat in Christina's breakfast nook.

"I'm feeling great, aren't you? I love being pregnant."

"Me too. And John is so excited. He adores Allison and Allene, but he's all puffed up that this one's a boy."

"So is Brad. And now me too."

"I never worried about you. I knew when you felt your baby moving you'd be okay."

"Smarty." Christina pushed again into Sarah. "I'm so grateful I got pregnant when I did. Waiting for Zachary has helped me to start living again."

"And it's good to have my best bud back," Sarah said, shaking her head no to Christina's offer of another warm cinnamon bun. "My ob-gyn says I'm not gaining as much as I should, but it's because I'm not that hungry."

"My God, I wish I could say that," Christina said, tearing off another piece of the bun. "I'm hungry all the time. Mother says it's because I lost so much weight after Sam."

"You're also biking almost every day so you're burning calories. No wonder you're hungry."

"No more talking about food or I'll finish this damn bun," Christina said pushing away the plate. "Besides, I want to tell you about my volunteering at Fellow Travelers. It's been another step up the ladder for me. I know I'll have to give it up when Zachary arrives, but for now it's what I most want to do." Christina placed the fabric samples back in the box and went to the kitchen for more herbal tea.

"It's turned me around," she continued, handing Sarah a mug. "I just can't keep up my Why God chatter when I look into the worn sagging faces of men and women dressed in layers of rags who probably spent the night living under a bridge or in a cardboard box. My God, Sarah, you should meet some of these people.

"This morning when I asked Harry, one of our regulars, how it was going, do you know what he did? Gave me this enormous smile through raw chapped lips, front teeth missing—like he didn't have a care in the world—and said, 'Not too bad, not too bad, another good day.' How can I not be humbled by that?

"And Rose—another one who brings me to my knees. She's this little old lady who walks at a slant, her hip is so bad. But today, when I asked her how her hip was, she reached over and patted my hand saying, 'Doing Honey. Now don't you worry.'"

"It's great to see you so excited." Sarah inched her body taller and placed a tan hand on Christina's wrist. "Christina, you have such a tender heart. Come to church with me on Sunday. African-Americans are big on a loving, forgiving God."

"Father must've preached some of that. But what stuck was the gloomy-doomy stuff. So I'm always twisting around the idea that God punished me through Sam. Mother says Father doesn't realize how his preaching and sternness have affected me. Well, I asked her the other day, when's he going to figure me out? He's had almost forty-three years."

"It's that you and he are so different. You're much more like your mother."

"Yeah, thank God for that. I used to wonder why she ever married him and even seemed happy with him but I've come to understand that she *likes* being the other side of the coin. Likes being able to smoothly slip in the right words—like placing a letter in an envelope— when he struggles with some part of his sermon. And I've watched the way she hesitates along the edges of something he's declaring as fact and then reaches over and takes his hand saying something like take your time with that one, Sweetheart."

"It's true," Sarah nodded. "Every couple has its own rhythm." She picked up the box of fabric samples and started to rise. Then sat back down.

"I should be going," she said, "but I want to quick tell you about a new second-grade friend of Allene's—a little girl I'd like you to meet. Her mother drops her off practically every afternoon to play with Allene and Allison. She's a sweet child but there's something about her that concerns me. When she takes off the sweater she usually wears I've noticed little pinch bruises—some are actually sores—on her arms."

Christina frowned. "Are we talking a call to CPS?"

"Not sure because yesterday I saw her actually pinching herself—little tiny nips above her elbows."

"Oh boy."

"Exactly. And I know as a psychologist you've seen everything."

"Next time she's there call me and I'll drop over."

"That'll be later today because they never play at Sandra's. Her mother just drops her off and picks her up. If I'm in the yard she keeps her window rolled up, clearly not interested in meeting me. Which I think is very odd—to drop off a child every day and not want to meet the mother where her child's playing."

"That in itself might tell us something. We always have to look at the context of any situation. I'll pop over around 3:30."

"Great. Thanks." Once again Sarah started to get up but saw Christina frowning. "What haven't you told me?"

"I didn't want to get into it. But you know me too well." Christina tore off another chuck of bun. "Things aren't right between Brad and me. He's as closed as a closet. I keep knocking at the door but he's not answering."

"Keep knocking. Men sometimes feel displaced by a pregnancy."

"I try, but . . ."

"Trust that the Lord will work on his heart and help him get past wherever he's stuck."

"Do you really and truly think there's a God up there Who cares for each and every one of us?"

"Absolutely. You know I do."

"But how is that possible? Think of the Callahans. It looks to me as though He's forgotten them."

"No. We just don't understand His plan. Right now we have to pray for them."

I wonder how much help that will be, Christina thought, but pushed back the words. Instead she said, "The TV keeps going over and over that little boy's kidnapping. It breaks my heart to see his parents begging for his return."

"Mine too. I wish there was something we could do to help."

Exactly one week earlier five year old Dakota Callahan had vanished from his front yard. His mother had run into the house with her other son for only a minute or two to put a band aid on his knee, and when she came back out Dakota was gone. Just like that. Gone. Paralyzing parents all over Connecticut.

"Maybe we should join the search group," Sarah

added. "I've been thinking about that but, when I mentioned it to John, he had a fit."

"No wonder! You've had better ideas. Think of it—two pregnant women ready to pop wandering around in the woods. But I'll tell you one thing," Christina added, "if I were in Mrs. Callahan's shoes I'd be screaming at all those reporters to stop clinging around my door like Saran."

"Me too."

Christina sighed, pushing a strand of hair behind her ear.

"My childhood friend Penny—you'll meet her pretty soon because she'd moving back from L.A.—is a Buddhist. And she says Buddhists don't believe there *is* a god out there managing things. They believe we each have a god-light inside."

"Like the seed Jesus teaches us about?"

"Maybe. But I haven't made that connection." Christina chewed on the last piece of bun. "At any rate, Pen thinks the teachings of Buddha about the inevitability of suffering in this life would help me accept Sam's death at a deeper level and would bring me spiritual peace."

Christina swallowed the bun and sipped her tea before adding, "But at least I'm back to being a rational adult—no longer a raging child cursing God. Of

course, we all suffer one time or another—that's funda-
mental. So Penny's wrong. I *do* understand that. It's just
that I still carry a shit-load of guilt."

"Christina! Please!" Sarah snapped her hand on the
table. "Sammy's death was an *accident*."

"Remember the gate?"

"An *accident*, Christina. Want to know the definition
of an accident?"

Christina dropped her head, shook it from side-to-
side.

"An accident, Christina, means *lack of intent*. You've
just said you're a rational adult. So stop and think. You
break a glass . . . it's an accident. You fall and fracture
your wrist . . . another accident. You don't tightly close
a gate . . . an accident. *No intention*."

Christina looked into Sarah's startling pale green
eyes flecked with gold, her heart-shaped face framed by
a bright red and gold wrap, and didn't want to contra-
dict her. She has such a good heart, Christina thought, I
don't want to disappoint her.

"I can tell by your face it's not getting in," Sarah
sighed. "So where are you right now?"

"Thinking about our differences. How you're so
calm, like a contented cat, always certain of God's hand
on everything, while I'm as jumpy as a frog." Christina
scraped her teeth along her bottom lip, moistened it

with her tongue, and bit again. "Then there's Penny. My childhood was a dream compared to hers. She was horribly abused and yet today she sails along like a ship under full sail while here I am, all too often feeling lost at sea."

"I guess I got my faith from my mother and my quiet disposition from my father. Dad's a pretty level-headed guy but I've also seen him lose it and I've had my share of turbulence as well."

"I never see it."

"It's there, believe me."

"Anything you want to talk about?"

"Sometime, but not now." Sarah blinked and placed her hand on Christina's. "We all have something, Christina. We all have something."

Christina nodded realizing that her light and airy friend had a nip in her wings.

"Anyway, I've got to get going. But hey, I love your new picture over the kitchen table. It's perfect in that spot—contrasts beautifully with your royal blue walls."

"Thanks. It's my biggest effort so far at matting and framing. It was quite a job because of the picture's size but I admit I'm pretty proud."

"You should be. But look, I'm off. "Don't forget about coming to church with us. We'll take you any Sunday."

"Thanks. I'll think about it, I promise."

"Okay. See you at 3:30. Enjoy your biking."

Christina grinned as she watched Sarah swinging across the lawn, hips swaying probably to a favorite tune.

She pulled out her ten speed balancing carefully as she adjusted her full body on the seat. Then, swinging down the driveway, she hummed her own rendition of *Free at Last, Free at Last. Thank God I'm Free at Last.*

She loved the sense of elation when she biked, as though endorphins were surging through her, strengthening her for what lay ahead. *My baby, my baby, I'm ready for you.*

As she pedaled past the old school house on Brownley Road she smirked remembering the weekends she and Larry, her post-college boyfriend, had spent biking the trails north and west of the school before returning to his flat and making love. *He made me feel good about myself,* she recalled. *Loved my hair, my body, my skin. What a high! For a while we were crazy about each other and couldn't get enough sex. But, like delicious candy, Larry melted in my mouth and then was gone. I sometimes wonder what happened to him.*

God, Christina thought, *must be the baby moving down lower making me horny. I know it's because I miss Brad. I try to give him the room he seems to need, but I feel empty like a glass upset on the table.*

Different from the day we got married, when I felt filled to over-flowing. Me in my long satin and lace gown, pearls stitched in swirls around the bodice and down the skirt, he in a dark gray tux, black tie and cummerbund, a beaming face. How we loved each other, she sighed. Even after three years of living together we still couldn't keep our hands off each other at the wedding reception.

CHAPTER 5

Christina and Sarah were still waiting. They swayed along, two waddling ducks, as their nine month bellies pulled them forward. But they were determined to keep walking. At least Christina was. She loved to be outdoors, to breathe in the fresh air whatever the weather, but she had to keep encouraging Sarah. "Come on, just one more time around the block."

"You're going to kill me, Girl. But you're right. We have to do this. But it's so *cold*!"

"Yeah," said Christina, "but isn't it beautiful today— the way the sun bounces off the snow? Reminds me of the fun I had sledding on my grandparents' farm in Pennsylvania. There were hills on all sides of their property and I never tired of the thrill in my stomach as I whipped down the highest one."

"That's something I missed growing up in Georgia. A few light flakes would fall now and then, but nothing stuck. So I get a kick out of it when we take our girls to the park with their saucers. John's like a kid joining them with his beat-up Flexible Flyer but I just watch."

"You're kidding me! You *watch*? Well, when our boys are old enough I'm going to take you down on your first slide. It's something you shouldn't miss out on."

"If I'm not too chicken."

"We'll go down together on my old sled. You'll love it, believe me."

"If you say so. But it's time for cocoa. Come on in. I'm freezing and I'll build us a fire."

Christina shrugged out of her ski jacket and watched as Sarah worked. "Where did you learn to do that?"

"Pop taught me. He often made a fire to take the chill off our house on winter afternoons or on early mornings at our Oak Bluffs vacation home on The Vineyard."

"Well, you obviously have it aced."

"The secret is to warm the flue before lighting the fire and then to correctly stack the fire with crushed black and white newspaper and slivers of pinewood and kindling before adding the hardwood logs." When she was satisfied Sarah brushed the ash off her hands, pushed her bulging body up and into a straight backed chair, and sighed with pleasure as she sipped the cocoa. "Now tell me what you think about Sandra."

"I watched her carefully the last two afternoons and I believe she's suffering with an obsessive-compulsive disorder with a big name—dermatillomania. She picks at herself to relieve anxiety."

"Meaning?"

"It's an impulse disorder. Could be caused by something systemic—neurological or chemical. But in Sandra's case I think it's more likely induced by stress. What I saw was a highly vigilant child who continually watched you with your children. Twice when you asked the girls to quiet down I saw her go for the skin under her sleeve."

"But I don't remember raising my voice."

"You didn't. Just asked them to quiet down, once when you were on the phone, and once while we were talking. But that seemed to be enough to trigger Sandra's anxiety—probably about what you would do if they weren't quiet enough." Christina stood up and began pacing, pressing her hand on her lower back. "God, I hope this baby gets here soon."

"Tell me. Anything more about Sandra?"

"Only that, like many pickers, she may feel pressure at home to be perfect. And, if that's so, then tamping down her natural vitality and fearing punishment if she displeases would be more than enough to produce the tension and anxiety relieved by picking." ·

"Well her arms look terrible. Surely her mother sees the sores."

"Pickers have a knack for covering up with their clothing or with sneaking on their mother's make-up. So it could be that Mrs. Milton hasn't seen the sores— or—chooses *not* to see them. It's a very serious business because if the sores are deep enough and don't get treated they can become badly infected."

"So what do I do? The only time I see her mother is when she pulls up to either drop off or pick up Sandra. She seems determined not to get out and chat. And there's something more." Sarah stood up holding her belly at the bottom and began walking back and forth, back and forth. "On parents' morning at school yesterday it was Sandra's *dad* who showed up. I was disappointed because I'd hoped to finally meet her mother."

"Did you get to talk to him?"

"Just briefly. He seemed awkward, even shy, but he did thank me for befriending Sandra. I intended to invite his family for dinner but he left while I was still looking over Allene's math sheets."

Sarah shifted back onto her chair. "But here's the strangest thing of all. The name card on Sandra's desk read *Barbara* Milton."

"*Barbara*?"

"Yes. And, when I questioned the teacher, she said *Barbara's* the name Mrs. Milton had listed in the child's records. But, later when I questioned Sandra, she started to cry, insisting her real name is Sandra. She wouldn't say any more and began crying so hard my girls were freaking until I calmed everyone with cupcake therapy."

"Hm-m . . . God knows what that's about. I guess for now the best you can do is nurture Sandra when she's here with your girls. Looks like your home is her safe corner."

"I guess it's true—it takes a village. But," Sarah said, rising again, shrugging her shoulders and leaning against the side of the fireplace and arching her back to straighten it, "so far *the village* hasn't been too helpful in finding that little boy Dakota."

"True, but the Callahans must be relieved that the body the cops found in the woods the other day wasn't their son."

"Terrible. Now another family is suffering."

"And the authorities are worried there's a serial killer on the loose."

"That's even scarier." Sarah shuffled to the fridge, took out a bottle of grape juice and filled two glasses. "Meantime, I can't wait for this baby to get here. I think he's dropped because he's very quiet."

"Oh my God, Sarah! Look! Christina pulled out her

cell and dialed Brad. She got his machine. "Brad, pick up! Pick up! Damn. He's not answering."

"It's okay. I'll drive you to Mercy. Tell him your water broke and to meet you there."

CHAPTER 6

"He's beautiful, isn't he?" Christina and Brad were lying propped up in bed, their baby wrapped in a light blue receiving blanket was sleeping in Christina's arms. She snuggled him in closer, kissed his little head and threaded her fingers through his soft auburn fluff.

Brad smiled over at her as Zachary held fast to his finger. "He's perfect."

"I love you." Christina reached up and caressed Brad's cheek. "Thanks for taking such good care of us while I was recovering from the C-section. I was freaked out when they couldn't turn him."

"Me too. But look at him now—he's thriving! And there's something about seeing you with Zachary in your arms, to seeing how perfect he is, that moves me in ways I can't explain. Maybe birth brings out my feminine side. I don't know. But when I hold this little guy in my arms all my troubles seem to disappear."

This is all I want or need, Christina thought.

"When I look at him," Brad continued, "I want to do everything right—to hold him close without smothering him."

Christina nodded knowing how much smothering Brad had grown up with—at an intensity which had robbed him of a lot of self-confidence and what she called internal grounding. She couldn't even imagine what his childhood must've been like with his parents constantly hovering over him. But she was only too familiar with the way his broad shoulders would slowly hitch up as though clamped by clothespins when he was around his parents. And with the way his face would sharpen, the points of light in his eyes rocking back and forth like those of a trapped squirrel.

Thanksgiving with the Fletchers had been a wipeout. It'd started when Brad came smiling to the table with the turkey platter, the white meat and wings sloping down one side of a mound of candied fruit, the dark meat and legs down the other side.

"Brad dear," his mother had cooed, reaching out an arm jiggling with bracelets, "why didn't you bring in the whole turkey and carve it at the table the way we always do at home? Don't you remember? Dad always carves while we watch."

"That probably would've been more festive, Meredith," Christina interrupted as she walked over and rubbed Brad's shoulders, "but I was the one who asked Brad to carve it in the kitchen. It seemed less messy."

"Of course, Christina, if that's the way you wanted to do it. But you do remember, don't you Brad, how we always did it."

"Right, Mom. Pass the mashed, please."

The ball was rolling.

Miles immediately had piped up, "So . . . how 'bout the election?"

"What about it, Dad?"

"Well, Bush's clearly the man. You did vote for him, didn't you?"

"Nope. Voted for Gore. Who, as you know, actually won the popular vote."

"Ah-h, but they're still shaking it all out. You'll see—in the end they'll declare Bush the winner. And by God this country'll be a damn sight better off," Miles gloated, squash oozing from the corners of his mouth.

"I couldn't disagree more."

"Brad, listen to what your father has to say," Meredith chimed in, lopping her head toward her husband. "He's right on top of all things political."

"And so is Brad," Christina added.

"You know I am, Son," Miles went on, ignoring

Christina. "Tell you what—let's look at what each man stands for."

"Fine with me."

Health care, education, immigration. There was no room for compromise, let alone agreement. Miles insisted. Meredith insisted. Brad resisted and then shut up. Christina felt wrung out even before dessert was served. God, she thought these two will smother poor Brad to death.

"It's unbelievable," she'd said to him as they were getting ready for bed, "the way your parents merge and swarm in on you."

"Always been that way. Makes me feel like a squeezed sponge."

"Oh Honey, come here." Christina drew him onto the bed beside her and pulled him close. "You're solid—anything but a sponge. Look at how successful you are. At how respected you are by your entire team. At how much you've accomplished." She wrapped her arms around his neck and pulled him further into her body. "Listen to me. Your parents live in a time warp. They can't see you as anything but a boy. It's ridiculous. I don't know how you can stand it."

But he pulled away from her. "Just leave me alone. There's nothing you can say to make me feel better, so stop trying."

"Oh Honey, come here."

"I told you. Leave me alone."

The beginning of the big freeze, Christina thought that Thanksgiving evening. It never fails. After he withdraws from his folks, he withdraws from me. Great. Just great. But I have to keep remembering the impact of his past if I want to understand how he is today. To forget his past and expect understanding would be as unproductive as planting plastic flowers and expecting a bloom.

But that was then and this is now, she thought. She eased the baby into his cradle on her side of her bed. Then buried herself in Brad's arms thinking we have Zachary now and things are perfect.

CHAPTER 7

"Penny, get in here! Look at you!" Christina threw her arms around the neck of her childhood friend, drawing in her familiar scent. "God, it's fantastic having you back from California. *Finally*, I might add."

"Well Babe, things happened fast after I nailed the job." And with that Penny swirled Christina around into the folds of her cashmere cape. "Oo-oo, it's delicious to see you."

"And God, Pen, you look as exotic as ever. Totally beautiful. I love the way you've pulled back your hair in that figure eight." Christina beamed at her oldest friend. "You look just like a *Sex and the City* girl. But no surprise. I remember how when we were kids you loved to mix stripes and polka dots and wore a pinafore when I was wearing shorts and tees."

"But look at *you*! Gorgeous—petite like a doll with your halo of red curls. Oh, ouch! Take these Dixie cups. They're burning my fingers." Penny swung out of her cape and pulled Christina into another hug. "Remember how we used to be called the red-haired twins?"

"Yeah. We milked that one pretty good," Christina chuckled, "until tenth grade when you dyed your hair maroon and stuck a fake diamond in your nose. No one ever called us twins again."

"Don't remind me. That was a tough time in my life."

"Yeah. I knew you were unhappy but I was too narcissistically adolescent to ask about the details. Just knew you had it bad at home."

Christina hung up Penny's cape in the hallway closet and pulled her toward the den. "I'm dying to hear more about your new job. Looks like getting your masters in social work has paid off."

"Actually, I think it was my minor in administration which carried me past the pack. But it was a long six months before the deal was sealed."

"You'll be terrific at the Renewal Center heading up the women's abuse program. It has a wonderful reputation and you'll blow them away."

"Planning on it, Babe." She swayed on her stilettos

and gave Christina a push. Giggling like six year olds they fell together onto the couch. Christina couldn't stop admiring her friend and ran a hand down the sleeve of her lime green silk blouse.

"Wow, Babe! What a gorgeous house! Oh my God, I love what you've done in here! The royal blue walls in the kitchen are so you. Looks like Brad's making big bucks."

"Yeah, he's doing okay. But he's turned into a complete workaholic—never here—and he's . . ."

"Uh-oh. Out with it Babe. What's going on?"

"Oh God, where do I start? But not now. Today it's all about you. I can see you're bursting."

"Am! Wait 'til you hear—I bought a house!"

"*What*? You just got in last night."

"Babe, I had too much going on wrapping up things in L.A. so I decided to let someone else do all the running around. Through Lance's connections I latched on to a super competent realtor gal. She did absolutely *everything*—faxed me pictures of nine, ten houses, inside, outside—'til I fell in love with *The One*. Then everything rolled along. All I had to do was board a plane yesterday and get here."

"You bought a house, sight unseen? *Without even sending me around to have a look*? How impulsive is that? Where is it?"

"In Southport."

"You're kidding! You can't get anything there under a mil. And you'd be lucky to get something for that."

"Chill, Babe. I fell into some money. Big money!"

"Come on! I know your family and . . ."

"Of course not. Got it from Lance."

"Your dream guy lover who broke your heart when he dumped you?"

"Dumped? That's too strong a word, Babe. But yes, he gave me the money."

"Enough to buy a house in Southport? And I'm just now hearing about it?"

"Wanted to surprise you when I got here. So Babe, don't be pissed."

"I *am* a little. Reminds me of the time you had sex with that girl with the long thick braid and never told me about it until it was all over. I couldn't believe it knowing how you've always loved big dicks."

"Oh, Babe. I've told you there's more than one way to get the job done. And she was one gorgeous woman. You should try it sometime."

"Yeah—when the moon glows red, white and blue."

"But anyway, sorry if I hurt your feelings." Penny put her arm round Christina's shoulders. "Come here. You know you've been my best bud since kindergarten." She flipped her hand toward the tall Dixies Christina had placed on the coffee table. "They're probably cold by now. But take a swig. It's chocolate raspberry latte. My latest addiction."

"Just go on. So Lance gave you a huge chunk of money. Sounds like a fairy tale." Christina sipped the latte. "Um-m, this's good. But I'm having a hard time grasping this money deal."

"Babe, that's because you've never fully understood the special connection Lance and I have. To him I'm more than big boobs and long legs."

"But he still dumped you."

"Not dumped. It was painful, yes, but I would call it an *evolved* good-bye." Penny shrugged and winked, then elbowed Christina. "Come on, Babe. Just listen.

"Here's what you don't get—Lance is a very unusual, special kind of guy. After we got beyond the initial steamy sex and he asked me why I bite my nails and why I have a hard time sitting still I knew he wanted to know the me behind the veil—that he wanted our relationship to be *reciprocal*—not the kind where I had to sit and listen to him talking on and on about himself.

"And as he got to know me in a real way—my child-hood, my hang-ups, my dreams—he began to urge me to go to his meditational meetings with him. I owe him for that because he was right—the Buddha's teachings *did* help me work through the childhood damage hang-ing on to me like dirt.

"In fact, Buddhism completely changed my life.

Without it, I'm not sure where I'd be today. Probably still bitter and faithless. I don't have to tell you—you were there. You know I was abused.

Christina reached toward Penny, cupped her chin with both hands, and looked into her friend's bright hazel eyes. "Of course I know, Pen. Maybe not all the details. But I know." How I love this wonderful, complex girl, Christina sighed, smoothing a few tendrils of Penny's hair which had slipped to both sides of her face. "But Pen, people just don't dole out. Money's the great greedy spot."

"Usually. But, again, Lance's different. He not only grew up with big money and with knowledge about how to make it grow. He also grew up with a sense of responsibility about how the money should be used. Babe, he's *brilliant*."

Christina smiled and shook her head indulgently, not knowing what would next come out of the mouth of her incandescent friend.

Penny took her last sip and placed her cup next to Christina's. "After college he enlarged his inheritance by funding the development of a variety of video games which he then installed in mall arcades across the country."

"Like the one downtown next to Century Sixteen?"

"Exactly. And he thinks those games will eventually

become available on small hand-held computers now in the process of being developed. And that's big, big money. So-o, Babe, just like that—like dropping a nickel on the table—he deposited five million dollars in a trust fund in my name."

"Oh, my God!"

"At first I refused. It felt too weird. Made me feel like a kept woman. But—see this?" Penny reached into her Gucci and pulled out a heart on a key chain. "From Tiffany's—sterling silver. When Lance gave it to me he said he hoped whenever I looked at it I'd remember how deeply I live in his heart even though we're no longer a couple. And he said if I didn't take the money I'd be participating in my own suffering which the Buddha warns us about."

"Wow! It's hard for me to grab hold of all of this."

"I know. Anyway, I accepted the money and that's how I was able to buy what you'll see is a magnificent property. Isn't that a kick?"

"Fantastic!"

"And there's one thing more. Lance knew I had no experience handling that kind of money so he set me up with his own broker."

"God Girl, sometimes I think if the sky were showering M & Ms you'd be there with cupped hands."

"Speaking of food—what do you have? I'm starved."

Christina laughed, then walked to the kitchen and pulled a dish from the fridge and a bag of chips and a bottle of red from the cabinet. "Luckily, knowing how you love to eat, I've made some guacamole. Bon appetite!"

"Oh God, I love this stuff." Penny ran a finger over the edge of the bowl, licked her finger and began dipping the chips. "So Babe, don't you want to know how Buddhism has changed my life?"

"Could I stop you from telling me?"

"Not a chance. First, as I've told you, it's about accepting suffering as a natural part of life."

"Got that."

"And, beyond that, it's all about how we live. Buddha teaches that *right thinking* leads to *right speech* which leads to *right actions*. Gradually that teaching helped me move away from victim thinking. I stopped raging about what had happened when I was a child and began focusing on what I could *learn* from what had happened. It took time but eventually I began to appreciate the strengths I'd drawn on to survive back then and, with Lance's help, came to realize how much I have to offer others."

"That's what helped you decide to go to graduate school for your MSW?"

"Exactly." Penny got up and twisted her body from side-to-side at the waist, then bent over and touched her

toes a few times. "I still feel stiff from that long flight."
Then she sat back down and eyed Christina carefully.

"So Babe, I've been thinking about what's going on
between you and Brad."

"Oh God. I knew your sniffer had picked something
up."

"So . . . I know he won't talk to you about Sammy
but I could tell from your face when I came in that
there's more."

"Well, for one thing, he's working longer and longer hours. Even some Saturdays. For another, lately I've
been catching a scent of perfume on his shirts. Then last
Wednesday I saw lipstick under his jaw. And now I'm
getting no-one-there hang-up calls."

"Hm-m . . . ."

"He claims he has to work those hours if he wants
the big promotion. But to me the signals are blinking."

"How's the old In and Out?"

"World's not spinning any more. It was great for a
while right after Zack was born but it didn't last. Now
it feels as though our dance is over."

"Okay. Long hours—even Saturdays. Perfume, lipstick, no one on the other end of the phone, sex a blah."
Penny rubbed her hands together as though wiping
them dry. "Good enough for me."

"I keep thinking I might be wrong."

"You're pathetic."

"Maybe." Christina pulled a tissue from her jeans pocket and blew.

"Babe, you're going to be surprised, but I've got some suspicions about Brad."

"And?"

"I've been thinking about the way he moves toward you for a while and then drifts away. And I've asked myself, what is it with all of that?"

"And?"

"And I come up with nothing. But Babe, it's weird. There's something very wrong going on with him."

"No kidding." Christina fiddled with her wedding ring, pushing it around and around. "Pen, I know you're good at studying the pieces of a puzzle and coming up with a picture, so when you get one let me know. Marlene thinks his withdrawal is a defense mechanism which is protecting him in a pretty major way ever since Sammy died and that he sorely needs his own therapy to work things out.

"I told her that'll be the day. But here's what I think . . . I think Brad's basically chosen to blot Sammy out of his mind. And, when he does that, he can move closer to me. But, when he can't blot Sam out, he gets angry at me and drifts away."

"See. That's where you're stuck. I think your guilt is preventing you from digging into what's *really* going on with Brad."

"So, great Guru, what do you suggest I do?"

"Stop focusing on yourself and start looking at Brad from a different angle."

"O-kay. But I can't picture how to do that." Christina swallowed and took a deep breath. She felt itchy inside— nervous, jittery. Penny noticed and decided for the moment to move on.

"So—when are you coming over to see my house? Like—how 'bout right now?"

"Can't. I have to feed Zack and get him settled for the night. But why don't you stay for dinner. I'm broiling lamb chops."

"Not tonight, Babe. I'm dying to get back to the house—to walk around each room—think about how to pull it all together. You know."

Christina nodded.

"But please! Promise you'll come over tomorrow. I can't wait 'til you see it! And by the way, Babe, I'm no longer Penny Darlisch. I've changed my name to Penny *Darling*. Isn't that a kick?"

"Sure is. What's with it?"

"Hated the name Darlisch and, since Lance always called me Penny darling, I decided to make it legal starting with the deed to my house. In big italic letters it reads *Penny Darling!* Tell me that's not a kick! "

CHAPTER 8

Christina walked with the chill in her heart into the warmth of her mother's kitchen and her mother's arms.

"Christina, what is it, Darling?"

"I'm in the dumps. I feel like an ungrateful wretch. Look at this gorgeous baby. He means the world to me and yet I'm unhappy."

"Come here, little love bug. Come to Grandma." Ellen cuddled the baby over her shoulder patting his back before snuggling him into the white bassinet around the corner in the dining room. "You came just as I was opening my order of scrapple from Deitzman's."

"Really? I didn't know you still ordered from them. My God! Pennsylvania Dutch scrapple! My mouth's already watering!"

"Please, Christina. Don't take the Lord's name in vain like that."

"Sorry, Mother. But I love scrapple! One of my best memories is spending that summer when I was eleven on Grandma's farm. She made me scrapple with fried potatoes and eggs every single morning and topped it off with shoofly pie."

"I have similar memories. Mom was a real cook."

As Christina watched her mother at the stove she tried to imagine what Ellen must've been like as a child. She couldn't match the photos she'd seen of a child swinging from a rope over the crick and diving from a rickety bridge, the girl they called Cookie, with the composed, quiet women she knew. Where did all that vibrancy go, she wondered, as she peeked in at Zachary now sound asleep in the bassinet Ellen had re-lined with quilted blue cotton.

But she loved her mother's calm and loved being there with her. Just the two of them. She thumbed the edge of the linen tablecloth—one of many her mother always used even on the kitchen table. She ran her forefinger over the delicate cross-stitching remember-ing all the evenings Ellen had sewn away while she did her homework and her father sat reading in his favorite Lazy Boy.

What had each of them been thinking while I

worked on my trig exercises, she wondered. What had their concerns been? How little a kid knows about those things, or even cares about them.

But I *do* remember how puzzled I was to see Mother crying the day the President got shot. Why, I'd wondered, would Mother cry about someone she doesn't even know? And I'd been even more amazed the next day when we returned home from church and Father went ballistic hearing that someone had shot the President's killer.

It was different when, during school vacations, Mother and I cried watching *As the World Turns*. These were people we knew and cared about, so of course we would get upset when something happened to Nancy or Bob or Lisa. But those people in Washington were strangers.

Christina smiled thinking about her girlish self.

"Here you go," Ellen said, bringing out a bowl of homemade potato salad, chow-chow (pickled veggies), and catsup before slipping three crisp slices of scrapple onto each of their plates.

Christina started to dig in but stopped as her mother bent her head. After grace Ellen reached toward the end of the table for a card from a small porcelain breadbox with a cross and the words *Daily Bread* on each side. "Let's see what our verse for today is," she said. "Good.

This is what the Lord wants us to think about—*He gives power to the faint, and to him who has no might he increases strength. Isaiah 40:29.*"

Christina stared at her plate and kept chewing.

"So Christina, it's very simple. You're in the dumps because you've been relying on yourself and yourself alone to get through some difficult times. You've forgotten that *real* strength comes from the Lord." Ellen reached over and loved her hand over her daughter's cheek. "Sweetheart, you have this beautiful baby and a good husband, but without the Lord you'll always feel empty."

"I don't know what to say."

"Say you'll start coming to services with me. Nothing would make your father happier."

"I can't, Mother. Father's too heavy for me." Christina shook her head and took another bite. "God, oops, sorry—this scrapple is to die for. But I *have* gone to church with Sarah a few times."

"Good. That's a start. But why won't you ever come to our church?"

"Because—well, because Father's message always feels too dark. I think listening to him all those years really messed me up. At least Sarah's preacher is upbeat and hopeful—someone I'm able to relate to."

"Oh Christina." Ellen put down her fork, wiped

her mouth with a napkin, and took a sip of water. "Your father's teachings were never meant to oppress you but to guide you toward the highest, best way to live your life."

"Well, they missed the mark. He was just too harsh with me. He scared me and I have a hard time getting past that."

"Now that you're a mother and especially as a psychologist you must realize how powerful a parent's impact is on each child."

"That's what I'm saying about Father."

"But I'm talking about *Robert's* parents—two of the most authoritarian people I've ever known. So what do you think he learned from them?"

At first Christina averted her eyes from her mother's pleading ones. But then looked directly at her. "I get it, Mother. So Father reared me with that same authoritarian energy. But it still doesn't change how I feel."

"And yet I know that, under all your confusion, in your heart of hearts you love him. But what you don't seem to understand is that he loves you very, very much."

Christina shrugged and nodded, glad her mother had moved to the stove and returned with coffee refills and dessert.

"Again, my lucky day. Molasses crumb pie. Yum."

"Cooking for you has always been easier than helping you deal with your father. But I know eventually you'll work it out and come to realize how much he loves you."

"I've always known you were there for me. But he and I can't seem to understand each other. Perfect example . . . One afternoon you were out somewhere. I was about four and decided to gather a bouquet from the lawn for Father. But, when I handed him the yellow flowers, he made a big scowling face and pushed his hand in the air saying, 'They're weeds, young lady, now put them in the garbage. And don't forget to press down the lid'. I was heartbroken and threw myself on the grass bawling. See?"

"Oh Christina—that's Robert's black and white side. And who knows what kind of burdens he was dealing with in the parish that day." She stroked Christina's hand. "Why didn't you tell me?"

"Oh Mother, I didn't want to upset you. You know how uncanny kids are about protecting their parents. To this day I remember the afternoon Penny and I found out Santa wasn't real and I begged her not to tell you. Because, I'd said, Mother always puts out cookies and milk for him on Christmas Eve and I don't want to disappoint her."

"Sweetheart!" Ellen bent and kissed her daughter's forehead. "That was so young and dear."

"Anyway, Father was just too hard for me to understand. You both taught me that faith without works is empty. And I think Father's *works* with me sucked."

"Now Christina . . ."

"Sorry, Mother, but when I get started about him I can't seem to stop."

"There's a lot about your father you don't know. He's an exceptionally good man and someday I hope you'll recognize that. Remember—just because you're right doesn't mean you *are* right."

"Like I haven't heard that before."

Ellen rested one elbow on the table, chin in her hand, her eyes loving her beautiful but sorrowful daughter. "What else is going on? Surely your mood isn't just about Robert."

"You're right. What I'm *really* worried about is that Brad no longer loves me. And I think he might be seeing someone else. There are signs. Yet the other morning when I begged him to tell me what's going on he kept right on shaving, his face as placid as if I'd merely said good morning."

Ellen sat quietly, knowing not to push the river.

"He was so loving and tender for a month or two after Zack was born. But he's started working longer and longer hours and comes home flat faced with nothing much to say. And, oh God, I hate to tell my mother this, but there's no sex. No sex at all. Not for weeks."

"There are often dry spells in a marriage, Christina."

Christina tried not to let her mother's words slide off her shoulders. "I know. I keep telling myself that. But something's not right. He still will never talk to me about Sammy and that leaves a sad silence between us. We had a blow-out about that a few weeks ago and afterward he began coming home later and later.

"What set me off this morning is that I received another of those no-one-there phone calls. To me that smells of another woman. And," she paused, "speaking of smelling, I've been picking up an unfamiliar scent on his shirts. So far I haven't said anything but it hurts to think he might be cheating. That's what *really* has me down."

Ellen nodded and picked up the baby who had begun to fuss.

"There's nothing much I can say, Christina. Except that now more than ever you need to draw on your faith to help you along."

"That's the problem. I don't seem to have much left. And recently I've been having these frightening dreams. One night I was in an RV with a missing tire plowing down a mountain. Another night I was a toothless little toddler being chased by Big Foot. And the next night I was a bear without claws fighting a tiger. Scared the shit—oops, sorry—out of me."

"You say you feel empty, like something's missing. I'm not a psychologist but I don't have to be one to see what your dreams are trying to tell you."

"Yeah—easy. I'm missing power."

"And where does *real* power come from? Think of today's verse."

"I just feel that *if* God's there, He's bustling about His business ignoring me and the load I'm carrying."

Ellen knew not to say the Lord never gives you more than you can bear. Instead, she said, "But something in your soul remembers how you once loved and trusted the Lord. I'm absolutely confident of that."

Christina focused her eyes on her empty plate. It was too much to look into her mother's clear eyes.

"Your early faith is still within you, Christina. Think of this. If you want the power of electricity in that lamp over there you have to reach out and turn the button. Now—don't laugh at my example—but think of this. If you want the power only the Lord can give you must reach inside and turn on your faith button."

"Oh Mother . . ."

Ellen pulled her daughter into her arms and whispered, "Remember, Christina, we are what we believe and you will find new strength if you renew your faith in the Lord and in His power.

"The words given to you for today are perfect for

where you're stuck: *He gives power to the faint and to him who has no might he increases strength.* I don't think it's an accident we drew that card."

CHAPTER 9

In Christina's dream Sammy had been calling for her. That's all she could remember.

Now, busy framing a new picture for the living room, she let herself open her golden box of memories. There Sammy was. She could see him sitting on the rug next to her, bits of melted chocolate dried on the front of his tee, knees scissored as he stuck tiny yellow Playdoh balls into his nose, one after the other, and then blew them out giggling as he rolled over on the floor.

Maybe, she thought, that's why Sammy was calling me in my dream—to draw me toward the memory box of happy pictures. Well, thank you, God. If You had Your hand in that I'll have to say good work.

I often think of Dakota Callahan's mother and wonder if she's been able to hold on to her faith better than

I. She was on TV this morning. What a burden she's carrying. Does she actually believe the district attorney's pledge that his team is continuing to do everything possible?

So much has been made of her family's Catholicism but, with Dakota gone all these months without a single break in the case, I wonder if her faith continues to give her consolation. I can't tell anything about her from the way she talks into the camera.

Yesterday, her voice quivering, she spoke directly to Dakota. 'We love you Sweetheart. We will never give up looking for you.'

Then today, her eyes burning red, she pleaded with his abductors, 'Please, please, bring our son home. We promise not to press charges.'

Why, Christina thought, does she even bother to say *that*. Everyone knows Connecticut and the Feds have a high standard of punishment for kidnapping. Well, she's desperate, that's why. But I felt sorry for Dakota's twin standing there with her, his face buried in her skirt. I guess she feels it's important to keep him in front of the cameras, to keep pointing out that Dakota looks exactly like Dylan and that both have tiny strawberry birthmarks on their left hands.

She sighed. Completing the framing would have to wait. She stood the picture against the wall and placed the mats on an empty book shelf. Mother will be here any minute. And damn there's the phone.

"Hi Christina. It's Larry. Larry Phelps."

"*Larry*?" What the hell, she thought. "My God, a voice from the past."

"Yeah. Surprised, right? I'm in Stamford for a seminar and thought we could get together. Maybe coffee? Tomorrow morning?"

"God, Larry. This's too weird. After all these years? Not a good idea. I'm married. Have a son." But she shivered at the sound of his husky voice.

"I know. Ran into Penny in L.A. about a year ago and she told me. But come on, Christina. What the hell? I'd really like to see you."

"So-o . . . Are you married?"

"Was. No more. And no kid. How 'bout it?"

"No Larry, not a good idea. Besides, tomorrow doesn't work for me."

"Okay, pick another time. I'll be around for three or four days."

"Larry . . ."

"Come on. I'll call again. Just for coffee."

She dropped the phone into its base, pushed her hair behind both ears, and slapped into a chair. My God! To call after all these years! But damn, she thought. The allure of his voice still gets to me. She gulped the last drop of cold coffee, telling herself she was making much too much of the call.

But no. Larry, balls big as ever, would know I'd be hooked. Shit. I don't need this right now. I know for sure what's on his mind. He doesn't just call me out of the blue for *coffee*. Thank God, there's Mother coming to babysit.

Ellen's eagerness to care for Zachary had turned out to be a bonus for both of them. Ellen got to have the baby all to herself a few hours three afternoons a week and that made it possible for Christina to accede to Penny's pressure to join the Renewal team as a part-time clinician.

"Working with those abused women has been great for me, Mother," Christina said. "Finally, I'm able to get my professional feet back in the water. Thank you so much for all you do."

"Oh Sweetheart, I live for these hours."

I'm one lucky duck, Christina thought, as she drove down Grove to Renewal. Penny was right. For now, working part-time is perfect for me. I love my clients but God, sometimes their level of stuckness drives me crazy. They have such a hard time recognizing the many ways they're being manipulated—physically, sexually, emotionally, economically. Even with the evidence on their bodies and the hurt in their souls they come back to Renewal six-seven times before they find the courage to leave.

Look at Jackie, Nicole, Mary, Clarice. All are from the posh towns on Connecticut's gold coast—Darien, Greenwich, New Canaan, Stamford. On the surface they are women I might've looked at admiringly in the mall, wishing I could be as tan and trim as they are with their gold chains nestled in the dimple of their throats, their clothes fitting like bark on a tree.

But, now I know. Under all of that they live in a paralysis of fear, unconsciously monitoring and compressing their words and actions to provide safety for themselves and their children. Every damn one of them is terrified about what her husband would do if she tries to leave. The two I worry about the most right now are Jackie and Nicole.

Jackie—what a mess. Sunday night her husband choked her and injured her back when he'd thrown her into their china cabinet. All because his steak wasn't broiled just so. The next day with bruises all over her throat she stared out blankly as the group discussed spousal abuse. Christina shook her head. She's a teacher, for God's sake, with two adolescent daughters, yet she cowers before this guy.

Same with Nicole. Christina's hands twitched on the steering wheel. She pushed her sunnies up on the bridge of her nose and brushed back a strand of hair that was bothering her cheek. Nicole—my God, her husband clocks her every move—where she goes, whom she's with, how long she'll be gone. And sex is a nightmare. He wants it when he wants it, the way he wants it, including anal sex which she abhors. If she dares to resist, he slams her to the floor excited by her terror that he'll permanently damage her pretty face.

These women have no safe corners, she thought.

Later, as Christina slipped into a booth at Friendly's, a stop she made each afternoon to decompress and write up her notes before going home, she found herself fretting some more over Nicole. I need to find a way to help her leave, she thought. Right now her fear of leaving out-weighs her fear of her husband's rage. But it's her third cycle at Renewal and I'm afraid if she doesn't make the move soon that guy will really hurt her and it won't be fixable.

"Put those glasses back on!" Christina, her cup in mid-air, looked up, distracted by the harsh voice of a tall stalk of a woman in the next booth. She was yanking her little daughter's wrist so hard it knocked the hamburger out of the child's hand. But that didn't stop her. She jerked the girl across the table, nailed her chin between her hands, and shoved the Coke-bottle glasses into her face. Then, with a ferocious frown, she pulled again at the child and whispered in her ear.

That's how it starts, Christina thought. Poor kid probably gets walloped at home. Just the kind who'll grow up and repeat the cycle—marrying an abusive husband and someday ending up at Renewal.

CHAPTER 10

Christina was bubbling over—pleased with how she'd mounted six of the best pictures she'd taken of Allene, Allison, and baby Alex, placing one shot of each child in a triangle and three others in an inverted triangle so that an attractive diamond had been formed. So she was stunned when, after Sarah tore open the birthday wrapping, her friend dissolved in tears.

"Sarah, what's wrong?" No answer. Only more sobbing. Christina told herself don't say a word. Don't move. Don't fiddle with your hands. Just wait. John had taken Allene and Allison to the Bronx Zoo and Ellen was caring for babies Zachary and Alex so the two women could celebrate Sarah's 43rd. But now, Christina thought, looks like we might not get to The Landing for lobster after all.

Finally Sarah looked up through dark wet lashes. "Oh Christina, I'm so sorry. But," she lowered her head, crossed her arms over her chest, "there are memories—ones I can tuck away most of the time—which can overwhelm me around my birthday."

Christina nodded, thinking, this's the nip in Sarah's wing.

Sarah moved a finger over the silver frame, circling each child again and again. "Two days before I turned thirteen I gave birth to and lost a beautiful baby boy. It's a family secret—one I've been wanting to talk to you about. And today must be the day because seeing my three little A's in your beautiful photo made me ache for Allen."

Christina moved over on the sofa and scooped Sarah into her arms. "Oh Sarah, for months you sat with me while I grieved Sammy. How on earth could you have done that with this behind you?"

"I could sit with you *because* of that. Actually, except for the few days round my June birthday and Allen's, I'm pretty much at peace about it although Allen's always in my heart and prayers. But when it happened I was a mess—even took an overdose and had to have my stomach pumped. I caused my parents a lot of pain."

"Oh my God, I'm so sorry." Christina took out a hankie and wiped the tears from Sarah's cheeks. Then took a deep breath and asked, "Was Allen stillborn or did he die of a congenital defect?"

"Neither." Sarah sat up straight and wiped her tears. "I had to give him up for adoption. Wasn't allowed a choice. After he was born I only got to hold him for five minutes. Then the nurse grabbed him and took him away. I never saw him again. He was beautiful—a tiny cocoa face and tight black curls like the boy's."

"What do you mean you weren't allowed a choice? He was *your* baby."

"But I was a child—two days short of thirteen and, even in loosey-goosey 1970, my parents considered my pregnancy a great disgrace. Christina, they had struggled hard to maintain upper middle-class status and I knew I couldn't embarrass them. So I kept my secret under bulky clothing until I could no longer ignore the fluttering and had to tell my mom.

"I was four months along and both Mom and Pop insisted I go away to a home for unwed mothers. My grandmom wanted me to stay home, have the baby, and let her help me raise it, but my parents wouldn't hear of it. Even though Grandmom pressed hard, reminding them that African-Americans look after their own, they held firm. The baby would be given away. That was final."

"Oh, my God!" Christina gently ran her hand across Sarah's shoulders.

"I knew I had to obey them."

"What about the baby's father?"

"A boy. Just a boy. Couldn't care less. Barely blinked. Stared down at the ground and said, 'Shit, that's your problem, Girl.' I pulled at his sleeve, cried, begged, remembering how when he'd pushed me on the grass behind our church—our *only* time—he kept whispering, 'I love you, Pretty Girl. I love you.'

"Mom cried and cried when I told them that and Pop stormed around the house banging anything he could get hold of. And, although Mom slept next to me holding me tight and telling me how much she loved me until I dozed off, she kept whispering 'Sweetheart, you have to let the baby go. There's no other way.'"

"You must've been scared to death."

"Totally. Pop drove me to this miserable boarding house type of place for unwed black girls in southern Georgia, a hundred miles or so south of where he had his dental practice. I imagine he'd heard a lot of stories in his office. After registering me with Mrs. Dixon, a combination housemother and social worker, he made me initial his signed authorization for the baby's adoption. Then he kissed me and drove away.

"Seven other girls were there and we knew each other only by first names. We weren't supposed to talk about *the event* but we did whisper. Still, I didn't learn enough.

"When my water broke I was mortified—thought I'd peed in bed. One of the girls called for Mrs. Dixon and she whisked me away."

"Oh my God." Christina wrapped her arms more tightly around Sarah. "How scary!"

"Unbelievably so! Anyway, as soon as I got to the hospital, the white attendants took my pink teddy bear and threw it in the waste can. Then they shaved me, gave me an enema, and rolled me into delivery where they put my legs in stirrups and belted my arms down—all pretty archaic. I was scared to death when they beamed a bright light into me and pushed my legs apart. I cried and cried in pain, not understanding a thing about how my baby was going to get out. The last thing I heard as they put a mask over my face was, 'You had your fun. Now pay your dues.'"

"That's unbelievable!"

"Terrible. I remember nothing about labor. Was completely knocked out by the anesthesia. One of the girls told me it would be like a big B.M., so I was shocked to find out where I was sore. Talk about dumb!"

"Good God, Sarah, you were only a child."

"The worst part was that I saw my baby only once. The nurse brought him to me in recovery while I was still throwing up, terribly sick from the anesthesia. I begged her to leave him with me until I felt better but, after only five minutes as I crushed Allen to my breast, she literally tore him out of my arms. And I'll never forget her parting words: 'Next time keep your legs together'. No matter how much I begged, I never saw Allen again.

"And I was never allowed to talk about him either. Pop set the rule as he drove me home two days later. I was sobbing 'I want my baby. Why can't I have my baby?' But Pop stared straight ahead, his face ashen and said, 'Now, now, Sarah. What's done is done and we'll never speak of it again.' I knew I had to obey.

"My heart's had a crack in it ever since and, when I saw your photo of Allene, Allison and Alex, it burst with longing for Allen."

"You poor baby." Christina kissed Sarah's cheek and wiped a tissue down the side. Then gentled her down on the sofa and covered her with a light throw while she went into the kitchen to make their favorite cream cheese, mashed avocado and tomato sandwiches on rye. She pulled out a bag of potato chips and started to make tea, but changed her mind and reached for a bottle of merlot.

Sarah lay quietly for about twenty minutes then sat up and reached for some chips.

"I don't even know what to say, Sarah. How did you ever have the courage to go back to school—to face everyone?"

"Well, Allen was born in June so I had two months before seventh grade. But I was in bad shape the whole summer and, three nights before school started, I swallowed a bunch of pills from the medicine chest—didn't even know what they were.

"I never saw Mom and Pop as mad as when I did that. When they'd learned I was pregnant they stuffed their hurt and anger and got me to the home as quickly as possible. But when I tried to kill myself they went crazy. I was grounded for three months. Couldn't do anything but go to school. As far as they were concerned Allen had never existed and Grandmom honored their wishes.

"But I suffered every day remembering the tiny body I'd carried inside the previous spring. And my longing for Allen pinched around my neck like a choke collar.

"Of course none of the girls asked where I'd been because, naturally, the boy had bragged. I was so lonely—pretty much shut down—and never developed any close girlfriends during junior or senior high. And I rarely dated because I was sure the boys thought I was easy. Which was a laugh because for me sex was a hideous burden. Until I met John in college and then everything changed.

"Kaboom. Right away we fell for each other. And I made up my mind to tell him everything even if it turned him away. But that wasn't John. He held me close, told me it didn't matter, and asked me to tell him all about it. Every detail. That's when I began to heal. And a year later for the second time in my life I had sex—*real* sex on our wedding night. Now you know why I love John so much."

"Of course I know. And I love you too, Sarah. You are such a good, good person. I ache hearing about what you went through."

The two women sat quietly eating their sandwiches for a few minutes before Christina added, "When Sammy died your strength helped to carry me through. I don't know how I would've made it without you. What can I possibly do now to help you?"

"I want you to help me find Allen."

Christina's face brightened. "Oh, that'll be easy! A web search should quickly get us on our way."

"That's what I thought. But I'm totally computer phobic."

"I'll get right on it."

"That'll help me a lot. I think if I can see him, know how he's turned out, the last piece will fall into place."

Christina raised her glass. "Here's to finding your son."

"What if he doesn't want to see me?"

"Always a possibility. Some adoptees long to find

their birth mothers. Others want nothing to do with someone they think abandoned them. I guess a lot will depend upon how big a void Allen feels about not knowing his roots." What Christina did *not* say was that in her experience men were less likely than women to want to meet their birth mothers.

"A void. That's what I feel—a void that's never been filled. No matter how much I love my other children, they constantly remind me of my lost child."

"Easy for me to understand. Having Zack makes me think of Sammy all the time. As mothers we can't help it. Our babies are in our bones."

"I know Allen's skin is dark like the boy's but I wonder how much in other ways he looks like my other three even though they're almost white."

"Was it tough for you and John in the beginning?"

"Yes and no. First of all, it took a bit of time for my family to adjust to the idea that I would be marrying white. And naturally, some of their worry about how we and our children would be treated rubbed off on us. But the certainty John and I had about our love carried us past that and over a lot of the early bumps. And it's gotten easier as the years have gone by because now there are a lot more interracial couples with mixed children. Although I admit—some people still do stare at me with my white children. I often wonder if they think I'm the nanny."

Christina itched with one burning question. "Sarah, with all you've been through, how have you been able to maintain your faith in a loving God?"

"I've had my ups and downs. In the early days just holding on to it by a thread. But somehow that thread was always strong enough to pull me along. Pastor Armistead is the one who ultimately really helped me. That's why I'm glad whenever you come to church with us. Pastor's such a wise man."

"How did he help?"

"By reminding me, helping me understand, that God doesn't push us around. He's given us the gift of free will. And with that gift we each make choices—some good, some not so good. It's *after* the choice is made— the action taken—that, through our faith, He helps us live with the results.

"So with Pastor's help I came to realize that, no matter how young I'd been, I still had *chosen* to lay down with the boy. God did not make that happen. It happened through my own choice. But it was the Lord who held my hand through all of it."

Christina nodded, thinking of *Footprints*. Then doubt showed its face. But if God doesn't push us around, she thought, then maybe He's nothing but an impotent Sky Guy after all. But I can never say that to Sarah. I see the bright light in her eyes trying to beam belief into me.

Instead she said, "Sarah, I'm deeply touched and you can count on me. I'll get on the computer tonight after I tuck in Zack. I know we'll be able to find Allen."

"I'll drink to that!"

"Me too." Christina straightened her shoulders and dipped her glass toward her friend.

CHAPTER 11

It was 3 a.m. Christina could hear Brad's tip-toes on the stairs. She pulled her robe around her shoulders and sat on the edge of the bed. The lamp was still off.

Brad slipped in and started to yank off his tie. Okay, here goes, Christina thought.

"Brad, I'm asking you straight out—who are you having an affair with?"

"*What*?"

"You heard me. No one works 'til this hour. I get it. You're sleeping with someone else."

"Tina, don't go crazy on me. I've been at my desk all night and I'm dead tired. There's a huge mess with one of my major accounts."

Yah dah, yah dah, Christina thought, turning on the lamp and jutting her chin up and forward. "Just cut the shit. Who are you sleeping with?"

"For God's sake, end it." But Christina could see the blood drain from his face, his eyes flash on high beam, as he slowly, deliberately kicked off his shoes, then stood glaring at her. "I'm totally pooped and need to get some sleep. But first I'm going down to pour myself a good stiff drink. God! You're unbelievable!"

And off he went flying down the stairs like an offended rooster, but she was biting at his heels. She had him and she wasn't easily going to let go.

"Brad, just admit you've got a girlfriend."

"God, I thought with the baby and your work at Renewal you'd have other things to occupy yourself with rather than obsessing about me and my job."

"This's not about your *job*! It's about your *infidelity*!"

"Come on! Cut me a break!"

"Cut *you* a break? What a laugh. You think I'm stupid? For weeks I've known you've been fooling around."

"For Christ's sake! Leave me alone. I don't have a girlfriend."

"Liar!"

Brad clutched his drink, shouldered past Christina and stormed into the bathroom off the kitchen locking the door.

Not to be out-maneuvered, Christina sat down on the floor and leaned against the door until she couldn't stop her head from bobbing and reluctantly went up to bed. But not before she pounded on the door hissing, "Hope your girlfriend doesn't mind cleaning up your puke every time you get the flu."

"Listen Babe," Penny warned the next morning, "you've got to start keeping track of all Brad's late nights, his long weekends and, for God's sake, start examining the credit card statements."

"I can't believe Brad'd be stupid enough to place girly charges on our joint card."

"You'd be surprised. Guys can be amazingly smug and careless. And, if you haven't done so already, you need to take half of the amounts in your joint checking and savings accounts and open ones in your own name."

"I hate to do it. Makes it seem as though we're really done."

"Duh!" Penny shifted on the kitchen stool and tapped both hands on the counter. "Come on, Babe, looks like he's been fooling around for some time. And listen, you also need to get a passport for Zack because once his name is in the data bank Brad won't be able to secure one if he gets the bright idea to take Zack out of the country."

"Really, Pen. That feels like such a stretch."

Penny stood up and took her sunnies from her purse. "I've got to get going but Babe, please, you need to cover all bases."

"Will do," Christina answered hugging Penny

goodbye. She started to head to the desk to look over her checkbook, then stopped. Fuck all of that right now, she thought. I'm sick of thinking, thinking.

She bundled Zachary into his new little bunting and drove to the Ladds to drop him off with her mother. Therapeutic shopping is definitely what I need right now, she thought. And today it won't be my usual T. J. Maxx or Marshall's. Today it's Sak's. God knows how much Brad's spending on his girly in the City. Which makes me overdue for a treat.

Moving through the perfume, Christina spotted a silk periwinkle blue halter and tried it on with a pair of washed designer jeans. She preened in front of the mirror thinking, I love the way these jeans curve around me. And wow—the halter smokes! Maybe I actually *do* still have IT.

She smiled smugly, then saw two high school girls glancing over at her, the taller one elbowing her friend. Shit, what's with them, she wondered. Ah, what do they know—two chicks barely hatched? Personally, I think I could pass for thirty-five.

CHAPTER 12

"Father!" Christina was surprised to see Robert Ladd standing at her front door. "Come in, come in. It's chilly out there. Are you okay?"

"Of course I am, Christina. I hope I came at a good time. Your mother told me Zachary usually naps around two."

"I put him down about ten minutes ago." She took his coat and hung it in the closet and placed his hat on a shelf. "I just pulled a tray of chocolate chips from the oven, so it's a great time."

Christina's head was buzzing with why. Her father rarely came over by himself. She filled two coffee mugs, piled cookies on a plate, and settled across from him at the kitchen table, one hand flicking a dot of flour from her eyebrow.

"So Father, it's good to see you. Is something wrong with Mother?"

"No, it's not Ellen. But . . ." He pianoed his fingers on the edge of the placemat. "Christina, there's something I need to tell you. I've been putting it off for a long time—too long, hoping things would resolve themselves and I wouldn't have to get involved."

"My God . . . oops, sorry. What *is* it?"

"First, I've been very concerned about how much you still carry around about Sammy." He paused and ever so slightly turned his head sideways as he took his daughter's hand. "I know you don't want me to say this, Child, but you need to stop blaming God."

Ordinarily Christina would've bristled, but there was something touching about her father dropping by like this, by the unusual gentleness in his tone, by the way his hand rested softly around hers. So she nodded recognizing that his energy felt entirely different from when he'd sat her down as a child. When he'd said God doesn't like little girls who refuse to put on ski pants even though it's zero outside. Or when he'd said God would be unhappy with a surly little girl who fusses every single day about practicing the piano for an hour.

Robert continued. "First of all, Christina, I want to talk to you about free will."

Oh boy, Christina thought, tightening up. He and

Sarah are birds on the same fence. But when Sarah talks to me I can hear. Not so sure about it when it's Father."

"Imagine this . . ." Her father finished a cookie, then spread his hands out wide and moved them back and forth sideways, palms facing Christina.

"Imagine you're sitting in your yard on a lawn chair. Pretend your yard's enclosed by a seven foot brick wall. Do you think, from your lawn chair, you could see over that wall into your neighbor's yard?"

"Of course not. The wall would make it physically impossible." Christina shifted guardedly.

"Exactly," he said. "You'd only be able to see into your neighbor's yard from a second floor window. Because seeing over a seven foot brick wall from ground level is *intrinsically impossible*. And no amount of prayer would change that circumstance. Because God doesn't operate in opposition to the laws of nature. To expect Him to do so would be nonsense and contrary to our having free will."

"Okay. But . . ."

"Christina, I'm giving you that example for a reason." She scanned her father's earnest face and his fidgeting hands—fingers tenting, then tapping one, two, three, one, two, three. And noticed his legs tightly crossed all the way up to his crotch as though he was trying to keep everything under wraps. But he continued.

"The only way Christina, it would've been possible for Sammy to have been spared was if the loose latch on your gate had been fixed. His flying through that gate had nothing to do with God."

Christina frowned. "What? *What* are you saying?"

"You see, a week before Sammy died, I stopped by one evening around eight to drop off copies of that month's sermons as I always do. I never know if you read them but I bring them over anyway. You were out running errands so I mentioned to Brad that the latch on the gate was loose and needed to be repaired. He promised to fix it."

"*What?*"

"Christina, I looked at that latch after the accident and it had never been fixed."

Christina's face drained. "Are you telling me Sam flew into the street not because I didn't pull the gate closed but because it *couldn't* be closed? Because Brad had never repaired it?"

"Yes. That's why you must stop blaming the Lord."

She ignored that last part. "And you're telling me *now*, after all this time has gone by?"

"Yes."

She shot out of her chair like a lit match and flew around the table to her father's side, swooping in so they were face-to-face. She grabbed his arm at the elbow, then loosened it as she felt its boniness. "I can't believe this! It's a nightmare! And right now I can't tell who's more screwed up—you or Brad. Are you crazy waiting this long to tell me?"

"I made a huge mistake and I'm deeply sorry. But in the beginning when everything came crashing down—you were raw with grief and Brad was furious and drunk—I didn't think I should add one more thing that would put you two at odds. Then when you got pregnant I was sure Brad would finally tell you—that he would want to clear up things between you two."

"Until suddenly you woke up?" Christina snorted.

"Yes. I kept praying that Brad would tell you. Then yesterday at lunch when Ellen told me how bad things still are between you two and between you and the Lord I finally told her about the gate."

"For the *first time*? You never had even told Mother about the gate?"

"No.

"No wonder I can't understand you!" Anger stormed through Christina's head. She paced up and down in front of the stove and fridge, round and round the table until finally she collapsed on the chair next to her father's. "What's with your brain? It doesn't seem to work in a normal way. My God! You saw me in misery but said nothing? How can I possibly understand that?"

"I kept praying for Brad to come forward."

"That makes no sense to me. Coming forward is what *you* should have done. You should have *immediately* told me about the gate. It's an A B C."

"That's what your mother said. She knows how conscientious I am as a pastor about keeping private the information I have about another person, but she's angry with me for carrying that too far when it came to you, my own daughter." Robert pressed the fingers of his right hand over his eyelids and rolled his head back and forth.

"Christina, I'm so sorry. I was wrong. Very wrong. It's a humbling lesson about how being right isn't always right. I've always felt you had too proud a spine. So I've prayed that the loss of Sammy would soften you and bring you to the Lord. But I was wrong. Instead you moved farther away. *I've* been the one with the too-proud spine.

"My God. How am I supposed to handle such irrationality? That's like thinking if someone stole my car I'd like the thief even more." Christina paced round and round. Then pointed her finger at her father. "And all this time you never worried about how I was blaming myself?"

"Of course I worried. But worry without action is useless and I had completely lost my compass as far as you're concerned." He dropped his head. "Maybe I never had a compass."

How do I deal with such craziness, she wondered. Then she looked at her father's sad face. Saw how he held his coffee mug with both hands like a child and realized he'd become an old man—almost eighty-five. His face with the high cheekbones looked sunken, his skin pale without its usual high color, his lips pinched as though drawn together by a drawstring.

The psychologist part of her pulled on her daughter part. She paced back and forth, back and forth, before the pull took hold. *Sometimes there's a moment*, she thought. And this may be my only moment with my father.

She righted the chair she'd overturned and pushed it next to him and sat back down. She took his hand. I have to do this, she thought. "I have a hard time figuring you out, Father, but I can see you truly believed holding back was the best thing to do. I don't actually get it but I see that's what you thought. I *do* see that."

She was shaken to see tears inching down his stern cheeks. Neither spoke for a long time as they sat holding hands. Then a source deep within her urged, you have to say still more. "Father, I forgive you. I know you weren't acting from a mean place."

He sat quietly for a few minutes, his head bowed.

"That means the world to me, Christina. And I want you to know how very much I've always loved you. Ellen's told me you don't really know that."

A first, she thought.

"You've been such a blessing in my life, but I guess I never knew how to be easy on you. I felt it was my duty to keep you on the straight and narrow as my folks did with me."

"I *can* understand that. It's so easy to repeat a parent's pattern. Now you have to help me with Brad." My God, she thought, I'm actually asking *Father* for help. Another first.

More tears rolled down Robert's face. Christina kept her hand in his and didn't budge. Only when the moment seemed ready, did she stand to refill their mugs. The clamp which had been wrenching her stomach was relaxing and, as she sat back down and closed her eyes to re-group, she felt a new, special warmth for her father. Hm-m, she thought.

"Pray with me, Christina."

It *has* been the moment for us, Christina thought, as she squeezed his hand.

When Robert looked up he said, "I know you're going to be very angry with Brad. But remember, Christina, anger has sharp teeth and you mustn't let it chew away at all the good things you and Brad have had together."

"Oh, Father . . ." She hadn't the heart to tell him about 3 a.m.

CHAPTER 13

Christina thought about what her father had said about anger having sharp teeth but she couldn't calm herself. Brad's betrayal was too deep. Too intense.

She knelt beside the den couch and pounded pillow-after-pillow, spitting out obscenities—cursing Brad's deceit and how it had lain coiled like a snake inside their marriage. She didn't even think of blaming God. Brad was the only one. What a wimpy chicken-shit! Rage poured out of her fists until, drenched in sweat, she buried her face in an afghan and collapsed on the rug.

She had lost her first child and now her husband. She felt she could never forgive Brad regardless of what her father had cautioned. I just can't do it, she thought. But oh, I can't fool myself. I'll miss his old sweetness—the sweetness he covered me with the years before Sammy.

And that wonderful dimple in his right cheek . . . How I'll miss kissing that.

She slapped her forehead. What's with me? I must be crazy. All the long months he sneaked around about the gate. How cruel was that? I'm done. Period.

She went into the kitchen and took down all the jars and cans, spraying Fantastic on the shelving liners, then wiping every jar and can before putting each back. Next, she emptied the silverware drawer letting the knives, forks, and spoons bang on the counter, some to the floor. She didn't care. She took a sponge and cleaned off crumbs which had settled in the dividers. As she was deciding whether she cared enough to wash the fallen silverware she heard the garage door opening and closing and swept the remaining silverware to the floor.

"What's going on? I heard a crash."

"You're lucky I don't tear your hair out!"

"Whoa! Hold on! What's going on?"

"What's going on is that Father came over today and told me about the gate! *That's* what's going on, you chicken-shit!"

"Oh, my God!" Brad dropped his briefcase and slumped into a chair. "Oh my God, Christina, I'm so sorry."

"*Sorry*? *Sorry*? You think that'll cover it? She nosed into his face.

"What else can I say? It's been eating away at me but I was too scared to tell you."

"But you felt okay knowing I was blaming myself? How screwed up is that? You felt okay letting me suffer—depressed, guilty—all the while you knew *you* were to blame? You felt okay about the nights I bawled and you said nothing? Okay about all the times I begged you to talk and you wouldn't? How can I possibly comprehend all of that?"

"Please, Tia . . ."

"Cut out the Tia. You've lost the right to call me by our Sammy name. Not after this! We're totally done. I can't stand the sight of you. Just pack a bag and go. The divorce papers will be in front of you by Monday."

"I told you I was too scared to tell you."

"Didn't you ever stop to think that if you'd told me immediately we could've shared the burden together? But no! You were too scared!

"*Too scared*! I'll tell you what too scared *really* is. Too scared is being a two and a half year old seeing a huge SUV barreling down to pound him into the macadam. That's what too scared *really* is!"

"Please, Tia . . ."

"Just don't. For God's sake, who do you take your instructions from—Snap, Crackle, and Pop?"

"Come on. We can work this out. Please."

"It's too late. Besides, don't forget I know you've been messing around. Just go." Which he did.

Pathetic, Christina thought. But my heart is breaking.

"So where does that leave me?" Christina asked Marlene the next day in therapy.

"Where *does* it leave you? Marlene asked.

"Heartbroken. I loved Brad so much. But I'm also relieved because a huge load has been lifted."

Marlene nodded.

"And don't ask me to pound a pillow. Been there. Done that. I'll probably be working with you forever on all this rage I have about Brad. I just can't do it today. I'm wrung out."

"But you're here. What do you want to work on?"

"I want to talk to you about Father. Do you think it's possible that finally I'm really at peace with him?"

"How do you feel right now?"

"Calm. Easy about him. You know how he always made me feel like I was too much? How he told me I was a thick-in-the-head Dutchman no man would ever be able to stand? Well, the other day he was different. It was as though a lock inside him had been released softening him. For the first time ever he was able to tell me he loved me. And you know what? I believed him." She reached for a tissue. "He also said I was a gift to him. Can you believe that?"

"I see that coming to you was an enormously humbling step for him. And that, when he let his guard down and was real with you, he started a reciprocal movement within yourself, making you able to open your heart to him with forgiveness. Which made him able to express his love for you in a way he'd never before been able to do."

"It's like magic. I'm blown away by how good I feel. Totally different."

"The power of a parent's words—I'll always be in awe of what that does for a child no matter the age of the child."

"Right now I feel relieved and open to him. As though, when I said I forgive you, a lot of my negativity about him evaporated."

"Yes."

"Father is who he is—a victim of his own childhood—a complicated person not unlike myself. And he's certainly given me an on-the-ground lesson about the price of pride."

"Yes."

"So I'm pretty sure I'm good where he's concerned. If I still have some therapy to do about him in the future, I'll do it. But I know we'll be much closer with each other from now on."

"Yes."

"But there's still Brad. The hurt he's caused me twists like a screwdriver's working my stomach."

"Yes."

CHAPTER 14

Christina sipped her espresso at a table in the food court hoping the familiar jolt would work its magic. Instead, it made her jumpy in an uncomfortable way, rather than in a good get-up-and-go way. I should've known better, she thought. This is a terrible idea agreeing to meet Larry. My God, after twelve years, what can I be thinking?

Truth time, she thought. I'm lonely and actually I've been aching for a hook-up. It's as simple as that. Well, at least he suggested meeting in the crowded mall—less chance of running into anybody. Thoughtful of him. But, now that I'm here, I've got my head back on straight. We'll do some catching up and then I'll be on my way. I honest to God don't want to end up in some hotel room. What felt so spicy this morning has suddenly lost its savor.

She tapped her forefinger impatiently against her cup. Just like Larry to keep me waiting. Damn. I should leave. Then her eyes dropped down to see an itty-bitty gazing up at her. The baby was about thirteen or fourteen months old and was fingering Christina's purse sitting on the floor. But as soon as she saw Christina smiling down at her she scooted away on chubby legs, the puff of her jet black hair tied with a purple bow bobbing as she sank into her mother's legs.

Her mother was cradling a newborn wrapped in a blue blanket and, as she chatted with a friend, she reached down to feed the little girl spoonfuls of rice. The child licked her lips swallowing some of the rice but quickly became distracted by the grains falling to the floor. Dropping down on all fours she examined the grains one-by-one trying with little success to pick some up. Finally tiring, she rolled over on her back cooing, da-da-da, her black bangs whispering above dark lashes.

Christina wondered how the mother could resist scooping her up and squeezing her to pieces. And her heart began to race, the thought brewing that maybe she was ready to adopt a little Chinese girl. Yes, when Zack's a little older, that'd be perfect—Zack and Laurel Rose. Wouldn't that be . . .

"Hel-lo, Christina. Look at you! Ravishing as ever!"

"Larry, my God, you startled me."

"Sorry I'm late. I had to take a last minute call from the Coast." He bent down and kissed her on the cheek his familiar scent luring her in. "Jesus, it's good to see you. I didn't know if I'd ever convince you to meet me, so thank you."

"I'm still not sure it's a good idea but, I have to say, you look great yourself." She smiled into his broad face, still youthful with its high forehead and sharply defined chin. Yes, she thought, I still could go for him.

"Here's the thing," he said, placing his cell and keys on the table, "on my last trip to Stamford a month or so ago after you refused to meet me I met an interesting woman one evening and began to date her."

Christina frowned, disappointment creeping into her chest.

"She's a great gal and she works with you at Renewal. It's Basheera."

"Wow, Basheera! One of our para-professionals. Small world."

"Yeah. It's like we're all on a plate of spaghetti curling into each other."

Christina swallowed the last bite of a carrot-raisin muffin and looked blankly over at him. "So Basheera . . ."

"Her daughter is enrolled in a charter school, the Tabet Academy, and has been complaining about some of the things she's being taught."

"Such as . . ."

"Such as the validity of creationism, the likelihood of extraterrestrials inhabiting our planet and, most disturbing to her daughter, a history curriculum slanted against democracy and our country. And her daughter says she gets put down by her macho-male teachers whenever she challenges any of those ideas.

"She was particularly upset last week because during history class the students were asked to assume Muslim names, to recite Islamic prayers in celebration of Ramadan, and to recite the Pledge of Allegiance substituting one nation under *God* with one nation under *Allah*."

"Do you have any idea why Basheera enrolled her child in such a school? I've never heard her talk about any of this." Christina squinted puzzled eyes over at Larry. "But then she's not on my treatment team."

"Apparently," he continued, "Tabet approaches high achieving students from middle schools and entices them to their academies with scholarships and promises of a first-class math and science education. But, now that the daughter understands what the curriculum is *really* like, she wants to transfer out. Problem is, she feels she can't because she needs the scholarship."

"So why are you telling me all of this?" Boy, she thought, this's certainly not what I expected.

"You disappointed?"

"God, you can still read my face." Christina could feel the heat rising but had to smile. "Well, what was I supposed to think when you call after all these years?"

"And you were right. I was definitely looking forward to an afternoon delight—maybe re-kindling what we once had. But then I met Basheera and now I have this new situation."

"New situation?"

"Yeah. My agency in D.C. where you and I met and worked together back in the early eighties has been suspicious of the Tabet Academies. And there are others like it operating under different names—all preaching radical Islam. So I've been thinking that you and I should delay our rendezvous."

"*Delay*!" Christina couldn't help laughing. "Still the same confident alpha male."

"It's gotten me this far." He reached over and took her hand. "And you *are* ravishing. And I hate delayed gratification, but . . ."

"But . . ."

"But for now if you could help with this academy situation I'd be in your debt."

"I don't want you in my debt." Christina removed her hand from under his. "Just spit it out. What do you want?"

"Basheera's told me that Tabet in Stamford is looking

for a psychologist. I know you're already part-time at Renewal but I'm wondering if you'd consider applying for the position at Tabet."

"To deepen the agency's inside knowledge of what's going on?"

"Exactly."

"God, Larry. I love my work at Renewal. Besides, Penny would have a fit if I left. There's been crisis-after-crisis these last few weeks."

"The thing is, my agency has become increasingly alarmed about this group since the 1993 bombing of the World Trade Center when a truck bomb intended to take down both towers detonated in a parking garage. Its ultimate mission failed although it created a one hundred foot crater, killing six people and injuring a thousand others. Four Islamic fundamentalists were tried, convicted and given life sentences for the bombing so we have good reason for being concerned about programs like Tabet's. They're hotbeds for radical Islamic teachings.

"Whoa, Larry. Shouldn't there be room in classrooms for controversial discussions?"

"Not when the teachings promote overthrow of democratic governments in the name of Allah." Larry leaned back in his chair and loosened his tie. "Christina, we're not talking about the Islamic academies which teach the inspirational aspects of Islam and foster universal brotherhood. We're talking about academies whose distorted teachings promote terrorism."

Christina absent-mindedly reached for a salt shaker and moved it back and forth. "How can you be sure of all of this?"

"Come on, Christina. You worked for our agency. You know how long its investigative arm is."

She nodded. Then shook her head no. "I can't help you, Larry. I don't want to leave Renewal. Although," she pinched her cheeks together with her left hand, "I admit the idea of a new challenge is fascinating."

He took off his glasses, rubbed his eyes. "What if you framed it as an opportunity to disclose a system which not only is dangerous to our nation's security but also covertly stigmatizes females? Anything concrete you could get for us would be important because Tabet now has its foothold in seven other states besides Connecticut. And we think parents deserve to know the precise goals and orientation of this group."

"Let me think it over. I just hate to leave Renewal."

"I'm going to be looking for a yes."

CHAPTER 15

Christina glared at Brad. "You want joint custody of Zack?" She snapped her face into his. "I'll never agree to that. When in God's name would you have time to take care of him? He's a *baby* and you think with your hours you'd be a dependable parent? How? Just tell me *how*!"

"I'll have to cut back, that's how."

"Right. Back from seventy hours to sixty. That would be just great for Zack. No way in hell will I even consider it."

"I've thought it through. I'll hire a nanny."

"A nanny? A nanny when Zack has full-time care with me?"

"Since you took that clinical position at wherever it is Penny works I don't see you as full-time with Zack."

"Renewal's part-time and you know that. And the three afternoons I work from two to five Zack's with Mother or with both of my parents—full-time with family. A thousand times better than being with a nanny."

Brad pushed his chair back and began pacing. "Christina, be reasonable. I need to have Zack with me in Manhattan at least every weekend. Come on. Give me a break."

"You work every Saturday."

"Now that I have my own apartment that'll change."

"So you won't be working, but you *will* be there with your girlfriend, right?"

"That's beside the point. And it's none of your business."

"Is. And it's on point. What's her name? How old is she?"

Brad's face was heating up, his Adam's apple wiggling. Stay calm, Christina told herself. Stay calm. "There's no sense lying any more, Brad. For my son to spend even one hour in your apartment I would have to know all about who will be there." She pinched her lips and puckered them. "But right now it's all hypothetical because Zack's far too little to be away from me."

Brad walked over and stood behind her chair, gave her shoulder a shove. "You're such a bitch. I've had it with you. My lawyer says I have equal rights and by God I'm going to get them. I want Zack on weekends and that's final. You'll be hearing from my lawyer tomorrow."

He grabbed his jacket and stormed out as Christina shouted, "And you'll be hearing from mine."

"Hello. Christina. This is Isabelle Jarvis." Oh my God, Christina thought. She of the golden chocolate eyes. "We met at the company party at the Plaza."

"Yes, of course. Hello, Isabelle." What the hell, she thought.

"I'm sorry to disturb you, but we're concerned about Brad. He was a no-show at our meeting this morning and Stamford told us he hasn't been in for two days."

God, what do I say? No one in the company must know Brad's moved out. "There's been an emergency with his parents," Christina lied. "I'll have him call you."

"Thank you. We're quite concerned."

Christina flopped on the couch in the family room, head spinning. This is beyond belief. Yesterday I found Visa charges at Tiffany's and now this. I can't believe he's still using our joint charge. And where the hell is he?

If Brad isn't doing it with Isabelle as I've suspected,

who *is* he doing it with? And where is he now? Probably off with his girly, the Tiff bracelet in his pocket. He must be smitten because skipping work is definitely not his style.

And wouldn't you know, now he won't show up tomorrow night to take care of Zack here at home over the weekend as he promised. Shows how reliable he'd be if I had consented to his having Zack in Manhattan. Means I'll have to cancel my trip to Chicago for the psych conference I'm registered for because Mother isn't available this weekend. Nice going, Brad. Just like you to leave me in the lurch.

I could check with his parents but I'm almost positive he's not there. And I don't want to give them any more to worry about. Especially Meredith.

I know she aches about the pending divorce. Neither she nor Miles can understand what's going on and I'm certainly not going to tell them about the infidelity because they probably wouldn't believe it and would turn against me. And I don't want that. They've been in my life a long time and, with all their flaws, they're family for Zack and I don't want to disrupt that.

Well, she thought as she re-dialed, until I know more I'll cover for him. "Isabelle, Brad said he did call in. I guess somehow his message got lost. He apologizes and says he'll be back in the office middle of next week."

God damn him! I'm sick and tired of his letting me down time and time again. What nerve. Putting me on the spot with Isabelle, causing me to cancel my seminar, charging the bracelet on our account. Who knows where the hell he is. It's a laugh to think he wants to have Zack on weekends. It'll never happen that's for sure.

The lying snake. Denying everything while right now he's probably circling his hands around his girly's ankles, caressing her calves, teasing her with his tongue as his hand reaches her warm waiting thighs. Pounding a pillow's definitely not going to cut it for me right now. But I've got to work off this steam before it's time to pick up Zack at Mother's.

Christina grabbed her purse and keys. Backing out of the garage she told herself to take a deep breath. Remember Zack and drive carefully, she cautioned. Traffic on the Merritt is pretty light this time of day. I'll drive up to New Haven, maybe stuff my face with pizza at that great place near the Yale campus. Their food's the best although I have to admit the place does have mixed memories for me.

After I got my license, she recalled, Pen and I used to drive there Fridays after school. Pen always made quite a hit with the Yalies in her skinny-ass bell bottoms and bursting sweater. The guys smiled at me but practically knocked each other over trying to edge into the booth next to Pen. Made me feel like Cinderella. But Pen couldn't help it. She's a male magnet. Always has been. Christina took a quick peak in the rear-view mirror and smiled. Lucky for me—recently *I've* been getting the eye. Well—at least from Larry. Not bad for a fortyish gal.

Now she kept her speed at fifty, all the while running scenes of ways to get even with Brad. In her best one she was slowly torturing him, snipping off his dick little-by-little, like slicing cucumbers. Make him suffer the worse way possible. That'd fix his girly too.

Oh, God, she thought, even I can see I'm totally crazed. Well, at least I'm just thinking this stuff. It's not like I'd ever do it like that woman out on Long Island. But jealously sure feels like a switchblade in the ribs. She took a deep breath and, after about thirty minutes as she could feel her anger folding back, she took the next exit, turning homeward on the country roads she loved.

But then the sorrow which was never far beneath her anger began to grip her and she turned into a Dairy Queen, tears spilling down her cheeks. Parking next to a Chevie, she noticed its bumper sticker—*Even a Hunter Will Not Kill a Bird that Comes to Him for Refuge*. That did it. She'd come to Brad for refuge over and over since Sammy and he couldn't or *wouldn't* provide it because he was too afraid to tell about the gate. Imagine that! Afraid! What a chicken-shit! And now he's doing someone else.

But, at this point, who cares? Oh, God, maybe I still do. She began to sob and pushed the button to close the windows, then let her stored-up sorrow pour into the emptiness of her car.

It took a while but, finally after her sobs had subsided, she thought, Marlene would be proud of me. Going to the depths *is* making me feel better. She reached over and picked off a small glossy card taped to her dashboard. Marlene had given it to her at their last session. Had asked her to meditate upon it—an R. D. Laing quote:

> The range of what we think and do is limited
> by what we fail to notice. And because we fail
> to notice what we fail to notice there is little
> we can do to change until we notice how failing to notice shapes our thoughts and deeds.

Well, she thought, right now I'm overloaded with noticing. Noticing that Brad is no longer the man I fell in love with. Noticing he's no longer the man I can trust. Noticing he's no longer someone I even know. That makes me finished. Period. I've said it before but now I really mean it.

My foot's on the pedal. From now on I'm doing everything I can to speed up the divorce. She took a deep breath, relaxed her arms in her lap, and placed her head on the dash. After a few minutes she heard her stomach growling, shifted the car into gear, and pulled up to the drive-through. This is perfect, she sighed. I'm ready for a Blizzard!

Sipping in the shade of an enormous maple, Christina finally loosened up, breathing slowly, inhaling for four, exhaling for eight. Breathing in I calm my body. Breathing out I smile. As always, she thought, mindful breathing helps clear my head.

I know I'm not going to really be healed until I can forgive Brad's cowardice. So much of that is rooted in the smothering he got as a child. My God, those childhood chains bind as tight as iron. I know if I can just focus on the lost boy within him I'll be able to forgive him more easily.

After all, our entire program at Renewal teaches about the power of forgiveness and the necessity of moving on from mistakes with better choices. So I better practice what I preach.

Which *doesn't* mean I forget the pain he's caused me. After all, my brain isn't a computer where I can press a delete button. But I must forgive him or the past will have too much control over me.

Right thinking, she nodded to herself—like the

Buddha teaches. But it's not going to happen all at once. She placed her empty cup in the holder, rested her head on the back of her seat and closed her eyes thinking, thank God, my rationality has returned.

When she opened her eyes she noticed a large *Framers Wanted* sign on a house across the road. Framing pictures, she thought. God, I'd love a job like that. Right now it would suit me fine.

She began imagining spending her days framing beautiful pictures. She could see herself helping customers pick out the mats which best complimented their pictures. Could see herself helping them decide upon the right frame. Could see herself skillfully cutting the mats, mitering the corners, positioning the pictures just so in the frames.

What a relief that job would be! Better than working at Renewal, she thought. Better than constantly reading psych journals to stay current. Just something to give my brain a rest for a few months until the divorce is worked out.

Why not, she asked herself. She flattened her cup and tossed it into a can. Then pulled across the road into the driveway. A compact muscular man in jeans and a tee with *Carter Construction* curved in a semi-circle over a line drawing of a house walked up smiling at her through her rolled-down window.

"Hi. I'm Chuck Carter. What can I do for you?"

"Um . . . Oh, God. I'm so embarrassed. I misunderstood your sign. I thought you were looking for someone to frame pictures, not frame houses."

"So you're a picture framer?"

"No, not really. I do it as a hobby. Sorry to have bothered you. God, I'm so embarrassed."

"Don't be. Besides, I have three pictures I'd love for you to frame."

Cheeks blazing. "No—it's just a hobby."

He smiled and tapped his hand on the door. "I've decided. I'll take a chance on you. The three I have were painted by my mother. And now that she's gone I've been meaning to have them framed. Come on in. Take a look at them."

"No, I've got to get going. Again, sorry to have bothered you."

"Tell you what," he thumped the door again with his tanned, open hand, "let me get them. See what you think." And off he went, his step confident, his whistle merry as a Christmas bell.

Christina could see right away he was a man of direct intentions and she fidgeted, weighing the pros and cons of backing out and speeding away. Then he was back.

"Here they are. Take a look." He positioned the first one on the hood, making it awkward for her not to get out and look.

"I like it," she conceded, "the soft, muted way your mother painted the children—almost like a dream sequence."

"That's her style exactly! Here look at this one." His broad smile pulled her in.

Two children were sifting sand into dump trucks, inner tubes tossed to the side next to shovels and pails. A young woman sat to the side under an umbrella, a book in her pink finger-nailed hands.

"It's lovely. You should be proud of her."

"I am! Here's my favorite." His thick eyebrows winged out over warm blue eyes.

"It's even dreamier. I like the delicate way she's captured the slope of the young girl's shoulders hunched over the piano."

"Great! So you'll frame them for me?" Christina felt she was losing her train of thought sensing his body beside her—strong, carved out of oak, his easy look encircling her.

"Well . . . if you're not in too much of a hurry."

"No hurry. Here you go. Take your time."

Flustered, moving too fast, she clutched the paintings he'd rolled up and tripped into her car, pumping the gas as quickly as she could.

"Hey! Wait! I should at least have your name and number."

"Christina Fletcher. I'm in the book—Bright Haven."

CHAPTER 16

Penny was outside waving, arms outstretched, hands flapping Christina's car into her curved driveway. She pulled open the car door as they parked, shining with excitement and grabbed hold of Sarah's arm. "Wait 'til you see everything!"

"Penny *Darling*, what's with the rhinestone tiara?" Christina pushed it back off Penny's forehead into her thick curls.

"Isn't it a kick? Well, I *am* queen of my very own castle, aren't I?"

"No one would doubt that! But the tiara doesn't exactly work with your bikini top and mini shorts."

"Lighten up, Babe. I've been sunning while I waited."

"Penny, this place is spectacular," Sarah said. She gazed wide-eyed seeing it for the first time, taking in the size of the sprawling ranch with its L-shaped wing facing a sparkling inlet where a kayak was lashed to the dock.

"Told you," said Christina. "You're looking at big, big bucks."

Inside, they marveled at the way Penny had used a minimalistic hand in decorating, careful not to distract from the spacious open floor plan with its cathedral ceilings, wide walls of glass, polished oak floors, and counter tops gleaming in black granite swirling with white in striking contrast to the brushed terra cotta walls.

"God Pen, great decorating job," Christina said, winging out her arms. "Beautiful blending of unique pieces of furniture in a mix of soft colors. I love what you've done."

"Thanks, Babe. You have a keen eye so that's a great compliment."

"I love all of it," added Sarah. "Just beautiful."

"Okay, enough oo's and ah's. Come on, I've lunch all set on the deck."

But Christina and Sarah couldn't help themselves. As they gathered around Penny's round glass table facing the inlet they oo'd and ah'd some more, awed by the beauty of the blue water, the maize sand, and the colorful flower beds strung along the border of the house.

"So here's where I want to bring you two up to

speed," Penny began, biting into her veggie panini, cheese dripping out the sides.

"Yesterday I formed a support committee to sharpen the search for Dakota Callahan, and I want you guys to help. I didn't have time to clue you in at work Babe, because every time I looked for you, you were with a client."

"My God, Penny, you've been working like a dog at Renewal. When have you had time to come up with this?"

"Our clients at Renewal gave me the idea. As you know, they're constantly talking about their fears for their own children. Here try these chips." She pushed a bowl towards Sarah. "They're sweet potatoes.

"Anyway, the Dakota thing has our clients feeling more insecure than usual, worrying about their own kids. And they're totally freaked that this one little boy has never been found after all this time."

"But aren't the police still working the case?" Sarah asked.

"Supposedly. I've talked to the chief and he assures me they're on it, but I wonder. So—you like the chips?"

Both women nodded and Christina asked, "What do you want us to do?"

"We need to put out new posters, maybe with a bright orange border. And that'll take a lot of running around because I want to post them in towns beyond here—around Hartford and further east."

"But they've already been posted all over the state."

"Babe, have you looked around Stamford? The posters have either been taken down or are all faded. So that's why we need to get up new ones."

Christina put down her panini, rested her elbows on the table and book-ended her cheeks. "Oh God, that's going to take so much time."

"Come on, Babe. If Zack were missing wouldn't you want people to keep looking for him?"

"Ouch. Of course. Okay. God Pen, I swear, you could coax a butterfly off a flower." She sighed, her arms bunched across her chest. "With my schedule this is *all* I can do. Next week I have a consult out at UConn. On my way to Storrs I'll pull off I-84 and put up posters in East Hartford and Manchester and another one on the bulletin board at the student union on the UConn campus."

"Terrific!"

"And," said Sarah, "my parents live in West Hartford so I'll do the same there and in Farmington and Simsbury."

"Great. I knew I could count on you guys. And that'll allow me to work with volunteers in this area. It's amazing how our women at Renewal—with all their struggles—want to help if we can get them transportation."

As Christina and Sarah were driving back home, Sarah broke their reverie saying, "Wait 'til you hear this. You were so excited earlier about taking me to see Penny's new house I decided to hold off telling you."

"What, for God's sake?"

"Last night the girls asked if Sandra could stay for dinner and of course I said yes. After we said grace John suggested we each describe something we're grateful for. And you'll never guess what Sandra said."

"Okay . . ."

"She said she was grateful her mother had Crystal. I asked, who's Crystal?"

"'My sister,'" she said.

Allene jumped at her, "'You don't have a sister.'"

"'Do too,'" the child replied.

"'Then why don't we ever see her?" Allison asked.

"'Because she died before I was born.'"

"I'm telling you, Christina, we all just sat there staring. No one knew what to say. Finally John placed his hand on Sandra's and said, 'Well, we're grateful you're here tonight with us.'"

"Oh my God! That's totally weird."

"Yeah. And, when the girls tried to ask more about Crystal, the poor child shook her head, her eyes tipping with tears. I had to give my girls the look and that was the end of it, but what do you think is going on over there?"

"A ton of tension. Looks like for Mrs. Milton Sandra is a not-good-enough replacement child. Think how she's even tried to change Sandra's name to Barbara."

"Now I'm more worried than ever about that little girl."

"Yeah. Poor child doesn't have what every child needs—a safe corner with her own mother."

Two afternoons later when Christina arrived at Renewal she found the staff devastated, the air vibrating with shock. Nicole had been murdered by her husband the night before. Shot in the head, dying instantly.

"That's one turkey who isn't going to get away with it," Penny told her staff. But that didn't relieve anybody.

They all wanted to wrap their arms more tightly around their other clients. Christina was especially worried about Jackie whose husband had knocked her unconscious earlier that week when he'd learned she'd consulted a divorce attorney.

"To hell with all the indirect stuff," she shot at Penny,

giving a rough pull down on her jacket and slamming folders on Penny's desk. "Jackie's in real danger. I'd like to offer her and her girls a refuge on the farm I inherited from my grandparents in Pennsylvania. Most of the year it just sits there unoccupied. I can have it cleaned and spruced up in one day. It would be perfect for them. It's a direct intervention I know, but do you want another one of our women killed?"

"No. But I *have* heard that fools rush in . . ." Penny stared at the ceiling for several moments, groaned and nosily clicked her thumb and third finger together several times before turning back to Christina. "Okay, Babe. I'm freaked too. Let's do it. *If* you can get Jackie to go. Something I wouldn't count on."

Jackie wept when she heard the offer. "I'll never get away with it. I'm sure he has someone following me. God, oh God, he'll kill us all."

Her two daughters moved to either side of her. The older started, "Mom, he's been punching you around for years. Don't you get it? He knocked you out the other night. Next time could be worse. We're scared to death."

"Sis's right. Do you know how many nights we lay awake crying, listening to him screaming at you, beating you? We can't take it anymore. *Please* let Christina help us."

"Mom, we'll make it work. We don't want to leave our friends, change schools, but we *have* to get you away."

Jackie twisted the cross on her chain. "He'll kill me, I'm telling you."

Christina took Jackie's hand. "Jackie, do this. For yourself and for your girls. You can do it. You'll never be sorry. He won't find you, I promise, but you have to move quickly when your husband feels secure thinking you're all in school. Do exactly as I say."

It happened quickly. Jackie wrote a note asking that the girls be excused at lunch-time for a dental appointment. Then faked a migraine at the school where she taught. The unmarked van picked them up on schedule and within minutes they were on their way to Pennsylvania.

Christina drove, holding Jackie's hand the entire trip trying to steady her as she gripped the sides of her seat and hyperventilated. The girls, seated in the back, were mostly quiet, now and then whispering about how they'd share the few clothes they'd jammed into their backpacks until they could figure out where to shop. Our plan's worked, Christina thought happily.

But after three and a half hours when she said, "We're almost there," Jackie grabbed her arm, her eyes frantic. "Christina, I can't do this. I have to go home. I *need* to get back!"

"Oh no, Mom, please!" the girls cried out together. "*Please!*"

"Jackie, going back will be a terrible mistake. You've already accomplished the hard part. You've gotten away. You'll be safe on my farm. Trust me. It'll be a safe corner for you and your girls."

"I just can't, Christina. I have to go home."

"No, you don't. Think about Nicole and what happened to her."

"It'll be different for me. I can make it work. Lately, I haven't been telling him how much I love him and that he's my number one. I'm sure it's hurt his feelings. That's where I've been wrong. He needs to feel more of my love. Please turn around."

"Take a deep breath," Christina said. "Think about the new start you can give your daughters and yourself. Think about what you'll face if you go back."

"And Mom, you *have* tried over and over. Please listen to Christina. Listen to us. We don't want to go back."

"Girls, this time it'll be different, I promise. Christina, please, take me home."

Christina had no choice. She turned the van around.

"Mom, we'll never get another chance. *Please!*"

"It'll be alright. You'll see. It's been my fault all along. I can try harder."

Christina bit her lip to keep from crying.

CHAPTER 17

When Sarah came in at six Christina immediately saw her downcast face. "What's up?"

"A letter from human services down in Georgia. They've located Allen but he doesn't want to see me—won't allow them to forward his address."

Christina put down her kitchen towel and embraced her friend. "I was afraid of something like this."

"That's bullshit," Penny barked. "You're not going to give up because of some lousy bureaucratic letter. They find him and now he won't see you? We'll see about that!"

Sarah's eyes jumped open.

"Too many women like you, Sarah, are forced for one reason or another to give up their babies. That's *huge* suffering. So this big concern for the feelings of adult children who have no idea what their birth mothers went through doesn't work for me. I say we roll out another plan."

"And I bet you have one," Christina grinned, sliding her eyes from Sarah to Penny.

"Look," Penny continued, hand raised, a fushia fingernail pointing at her two friends, "it's easier than you guys think. I'll call a private investigator I've worked with on two cases at Renewal. Put him on this. I'm one hundred percent sure he'll be able to work his way through the system and find Allen for you."

"Really? You're that sure?"

"No doubt at all. And it's going to happen quickly. This guy knows his way around a computer and the system. Someday we'll be able to locate people on the web ourselves, but we're not there yet."

"So he finds Allen," Christina put in, "then what?"

"Then we find a way for Sarah to accidentally meet him. Once my friend gets a photo of him and we know where he lives, where he works, there shouldn't be a problem."

"So we follow him? You sound like Miss Marple."

"Okay, so I'm Miss Marple. Anyway, Sarah might bump into him at McDonald's—or get in the same elevator with him at his place of business—whatever. We'll work it out. This dude is good. Believe me, he'll find Allen."

"But Penny, I don't like the idea of tricking Allen."

"For God's sake, Sarah, cut that out. All you want is a chance to see his face—get some impression of how he's turned out. I say you have that right as his mother. Period. End of story."

"Still . . ."

"Pen's right, Sarah. Give it up. This's your chance. Take it."

"Well, another thing. How much will this guy cost?"

"Again, not your problem," said Penny. "It's on me."

"I don't know if I can let you do that."

"Give that one up too. What good is all my money if I don't use it to help those I care for?"

"Well Pen, if you can pull this off, it'll be one incredibly good deed," Christina chuckled.

"I don't even know what to say," Sarah said. Just thank you, thank you, Penny. Your heart is huge."

"My God, Penny, I don't think your brain ever stops tick-tocking."

"Probably true, Babe. Now can we move on to something else?"

Uh-oh, Christina thought.

"I can't stop thinking about Dakota. He's been missing for far too long and the police still haven't come up with anything."

"Before you go any further with that," Sarah interrupted, "now that I know you think you can help me find my son, I have something else bothering me."

"Sure. Shoot." Penny said.

"Early this morning Mrs. Milton called to tell me we wouldn't be seeing *Barbara* anymore because her husband had stolen her."

"Stolen? She said he had *stolen* Sandra?" Christina asked.

"Her exact words. She said her husband had stolen Barbara. Had taken her to Portland to be near his parents. Then she couldn't resist adding that he is a total wimp and that he could have Barbara as far as she was concerned."

"Wow! That's some story. But, you know," Christina added, "it could be a blessing in disguise for that little girl. To be with the parent who loves her."

"True."

"Unless he's some kind of pervert."

"Oh, Christina. Let's not go there," Sarah cautioned.

"You're right. We don't have a clue about anything like that. But it's scary to think how kids get caught up in their parents' drama."

The three women looked at each other shaking their heads.

"It's unbelievable," Sarah finally said, "about what goes on behind closed doors."

"Yeah," replied Christina, taking a sip of chardonnay and pushing the bottle toward Penny. "I heard a lot of heavy-duty stuff listening to my mother consoling parishioners—listened to a lot of crying and agonizing. But then, the same people, Sunday-after-Sunday, would show up with big smiles on their faces—smiles I knew covered sorrow over a husband running away with a high school sweetheart, a child gone bad, bankruptcy, whatever."

"It's true," added Penny. "My God, look at our women at Renewal. Think about the happy faces they have to paste on to survive with their abusers."

"But then," asked Sarah, "don't we all cover up the shadows in our lives in order to live through things in some kind of normal way?"

Both women nodded. "Now I want to get back to Dakota," said Penny. "I'm not sure what the authorities *aren't* telling us."

"Do you think they've given him up for dead," Sarah asked.

"Maybe. Could be. Because personally I don't think they're doing much on the case anymore. And that bugs me because I have a hunch he's still out there."

"It's been so long. How can you possibly think that," Christina asked.

"A hunch. That's all. About ten years ago I lived in L.A. with this singer. A fabulous father. And when his daughter was kidnapped I thought he'd lose his mind.

But after a year they found her living in the next town. This's why I still keep hoping they'll find Dakota."

"But Pen, that's just one case. And Dakota's been gone a long time. Hundreds of children are murdered or carried away and are never heard from again."

"I know. I know. But I have to do this." She piled cheese on another cracker. "And remember, Dylan keeps insisting Dakota's alive. Says he'd feel it if his twin were dead."

"A six year old? You're latching onto a child's supposed intuition? A six year old? Isn't that a bit too oo-oo?"

"Not for me." Penny pulled a long yellow sheet from her briefcase. "Ladies, tomorrow I'm seeing the chief before I go into Renewal and I want you two to sign this petition urging him to step up the search." She handed each of them a pen.

"Looks like you've already got a lot of names," Christina said signing the sheet, then going into the kitchen.

"Yeah. I've been passing it around to everyone I know. I just feel led to do something to reignite the search."

Sarah saw Christina pulling a hot dish out of the oven and stood up to dim the dining room chandelier and to light two candles.

"Babe, everything looks wonderful. I'm starved."

"Me too." Sarah said. "When I first came in I didn't think I'd be able to swallow a drop but, thanks to you Penny, I'm revived."

"Wait 'til you taste this," Penny said, bobbing her fork dripping with a chunk of chicken. "Babe, your Pennsylvania Dutch potpie is fantastic!"

"Thanks. It did turn out pretty well, but I can never get the dumplings as smooth as Grandma's."

"Yum," said Sarah, "I've never had dandelion salad. It's delicious."

"Yeah. Another of Grandma's recipes. She taught me exactly how much bacon to blend in with the rest of the ingredients. Not too much she told me."

"You and she were very close, weren't you," Sarah asked.

"We were. That's why she left me the farm. She knew Mother was taken care of and she wanted me to have it as a cushion—knew how much I loved it. And I've kept everything just the way she had it so that as Zack and I go there he can share with me the experience of living with her furnishings from another era."

"And that also keeps you feeling close to her, doesn't it," asked Sarah.

"Absolutely. I love the plain maroon or flowered velvety material covering the couch and chairs, all with heavily carved arms. And I can see Zachary climbing on the dark oak hat rack, making faces the way I did in the oval mirror or lifting the lid of the leather seat and trying to fit into the basin designed for scarves and mittens."

"Too bad Jackie wouldn't take advantage of your offer."

"That was a heartache for me. And right now she's not doing well at all."

"Okay, no more shop talk," Penny said, "let's get to the shoofly pie."

"Help yourselves. I'll get the coffee." Christina stopped before she reached the kitchen. "There's the doorbell. If it's Brad I'll hit the ceiling. He's not supposed to drop by without calling."

She was dumbfounded to find Chuck Carter standing at the door, a grin wide as a slice of watermelon stretching across his face.

"I got your card that the pictures were ready. So I thought I'd drop by to pick them up."

"Um . . . Okay. Come on in. I'll get them."

Penny, jumping up, flagged him into the dining room and offered him a chair. By the time Christina got back with the pictures, heart beating all over her body, Penny was pouring him a cup of coffee.

"I see you've already met Penny and Sarah."

"I have. Sorry I barged into your party. It was impulsive of me. I should've called first."

"Oh, not at all," Penny swooned. "We're glad to meet you." She eyed him approvingly. Liked his tall but not too tall muscular frame. This's the guy for Babe, she thought. "So-o, you own your own construction company?"

"Penny . . ."

"Yeah. I inherited it from my father. None of my sisters were interested which I guess is normal. But of course they own shares. Anyway, expanding it and running it has pretty much consumed me the last few years."

"Awesome. And what do you do or fun?"

"Penny . . ."

"In the summer I do a lot of swimming and the rest of the year I try to bike almost every day. Would like to try a triathlon but to do that I'll have to start running."

"Awesome. Christina's bikes all the time and she was captain of our swim team back in high school."

"Penny . . ."

"Great!" Chuck smiled over at Christina fidgeting in the corner still holding the pictures. "Let's pull out bikes Saturday and ride around the reservoir. It's beautiful this time of year."

"Oh, I don't know. Zack and I may . . ."

"Your son? I'd like to meet him. We'll take him with us.

"No, he's only a baby. Um . . ."

"Think about it. I'll give you a call."

He thanked Christina for the framed paintings and, smiling broadly at Penny and Sarah, handed her a check from a toasty hand and breezed out.

"There you have it!" Penny ogled over at Sarah. "See what I mean? Look at her face! I told you she has the hots for her carpenter guy."

"Penny . . ."

"Remember how she talked about him, Sarah? His body strong as oak, his eyes deep blue?"

"Well, Christina," Sarah cautiously put in, "he *does* seem quite taken with you. What do you think—will you go biking with him Saturday?"

"God, I don't know. Can't seem to forget I'm still married."

"Yeah, and to what a guy! Anyway, you've filed the papers so you're practically divorced."

"What do you think, Sarah?"

"Not sure." Sarah bunched her lips together and loped her head to one side. Christina could see she was stuck on the still-married part.

"Good God. You two are going to drive me off a cliff! How often is a dream like Chuck Carter going to pop into your life? And Babe, you're way overdue for getting laid. You've already lost out on good-lay Larry. Chuck Carter looks like the guy for the job."

"I just don't know . . ."

"Have it your way. But personally I see him as a gift from the Universe."

"God Pen, you're so-o out there."

"Not. Seven years ago I thought I was HIV positive. Scared the living shit out of me. Then I learned the first test was a false positive. But, believe it or not, although I was giddy with relief I continued on my way—still sexually careless. Until, lucky for me, shortly thereafter I met Lance and began to study Buddhism. As I've told you before, he really saved me." She lifted her hands off the table and rocked them back and forth.

"When I began to meditate and *mindfully* reached out to the Universe as the Buddha teaches, I gradually found other ways of fulfilling myself besides sex, sex, sex—not that I ever stopped loving it. But I matured within myself and eventually set my sites on graduate school."

"So how does that relate to Chuck Carter and me?"

"Think about it. You've been working on yourself forever. My God, look at all your therapy! And, I think with your marriage on the rocks, you've been unconsciously reaching out for something or *someone*. Admit it, Babe—you were hopeful when you agreed to meet Larry. There's no question about it—when you reach out to the Universe you draw unexpected things to yourself."

"More oo-oo."

"No. I can see it clearly. Chuck Carter's a gift to you from the Universe. And he's hot. H-O-T, hot for you. It's a no brainer."

"I don't know . . ."

"Come on! Think about it. You're ready. It's written all over you."

Later, as Christina cleaned up the kitchen, she noodled over what Penny had said. Well, she thought, they say that at the right time the right teacher comes along. So maybe Pen's my teacher. Or at least one of them.

When she went upstairs she rooted through her closet. Then stepped on the scale.

CHAPTER 18

Christina had Zack in his car seat and was rushing to a concert Penny was sponsoring to benefit the search for Dakota Callahan when her cell rang. She saw it was her mother and decided to let it go. They were already late and she was looking forward to hearing the combined choirs from three local churches performing traditional favorites along with patriotic and inspirational pieces. It should be a Penny spectacular, she thought.

But her cell rang again just as she was pulling into a parking space. Damn, she muttered, I've got to pick this up even if we're late.

"Christina, your father's been taken to the hospital. He fell over getting up from his chair at the dinner table. The doctor says it was a heart attack."

"I'll be right there."

She rushed into Mercy, Zack bundled in her arms, and clasped her mother in a tight embrace. "Tell me exactly what happened, Mother."

"We had just finished our coffee. He'd been talking about an idea for his sermon. Even though he's now emeritus he still loves to be invited to preach once a month. Anyway, as he pushed back his chair to go to his study to write down his ideas, he fell onto the right arm of the chair and toppled down. I dialed 911 and Dr. Rothberg in a panic."

"God, Mother . . . sorry, you must've been so scared."

"I've been praying every minute."

"So where is he now?"

"They didn't fool around—immediately moved him from the ER to surgery."

"How long ago was that?"

"Seems like an eternity but I think it's been about forty minutes." Her mother slumped into the orange plastic chair and dropped her head to her daughter's shoulder. "Christina, what will I ever do without him?"

"You're jumping ahead too fast. Let's hear what the doctor has to say."

Within minutes, Dr. Rothberg was walking towards them, his head bent. Christina shivered, squeezed Zachary more tightly into her shoulder, and placed her other arm around her mother as they stood.

"Ellen, Christina, he had a massive heart attack. There was nothing we could do. But it happened so fast I can tell you he never felt a thing."

Christina pushed her mother back into the chair, grateful her parents' long-time doctor was there to break the news.

"Ellen, I'm so sorry. You and Robert have been married a long time and I know this is a shock. But after the funeral don't hesitate to come by and talk. Agnes will always fit you in."

Christina was numb with disbelief. Father, Father, she thought. Just as I finally was getting to know you. She wiped her eyes and blew into a tissue. Then she called Brad, confident that on an occasion like this she could count on him to handle everything.

"I have to give it to him," Penny said later. "Brad was a rock. Arranged everything for the viewing, the funeral, the burial. Sarah and I had little to do because the women at your father's church took care of all the food for the reception. My God, they had sandwiches and brownies up to the ceiling. We just made sure there was wine for those who wanted it. Didn't know how that would go down with the church ladies. And didn't care."

Christina found her father's death sadder than she would have imagined. At least Mother can find solace in believing Father's with the Lord, she thought.

Most of the day was a blur for her but ended in a beautifully unexpected way when Brad took her hand before they left the cemetery and led her over to Sammy's grave, a place she'd never once visited—the thought of him in the ground more than she could bear. But, as they stood at the tombstone etched with Sam's sweet face, she felt a surprising peace. And when she saw that small bushes with red berries had been planted on either side of the stone, she looked up in surprise at Brad.

"Mom takes care of things," he nodded.

Tears slippeded down Christina's cheeks. Surprised and grateful to be there with Brad, she squeezed his hand as the memory of their child encircled them.

Christina was stunned by her father's will. Not only by the substantial sum he left her mother but by the fifty thousand dollars he left her. Her parents had always lived modestly and tithed faithfully so she'd never imagined there'd be much of an estate. I guess Father was more financially savvy that I realized, she thought.

I definitely never knew that years before he'd made an arrangement to buy the manse from the church so that when he passed Mother would always have a home. Again, I see how little I understood about the way Father operated, she sighed. I guess he'll always be somewhat of a mystery to me.

When Christina commented on this to her mother at lunch one day a few weeks after the funeral, Ellen looked down at her napkin pressing and re-pressing the folds. Then, taking a deep breath, she placed her hand over Christina's.

Mother's hand on mine feels like home, Christina thought. Like no other hand in the world. Someday I won't have that hand and then what will I do? She felt a yearning—almost a greed—to savor her mother, her eyes, her smile, her warmth, all her details—store them inside like rich cream.

"Christina, there's a lot you don't know about your father. Here's a little caveat, for example." Ellen paused, slid her fingers together and raised them into a tent, elbows on the table. "Your father went along with me about ignoring your shop-lifting."

Christina's jaw dropped. "You *knew* about that?"

"Of course. Since when have you ever worn bright, bright nail polish like the dark red Revlon I found hidden in your sock drawer?

"You never said anything!"

"No, I didn't and I had to sit on your father about that. But I understood my good little girl sometimes had to color outside the lines—be a little naughty—to get something out of her system. The items were small and I trusted your heart, knowing it wouldn't take long for you to work it through and quit."

"My God! Oops—sorry Mother. But you were right. I only did that a few times. Thanks for understanding I had a valve to release. Pretty natural if you ask me. Because I think the first time I took anything was after Father reminded me that I was named after the Christ child and should behave accordingly. Can you imagine that?"

Ellen shook her head sadly. "Oh, Christina."

"Fortunately the shop-lifting only gave me a temporary boost of power and very soon Jiminy Cricket sitting on my shoulder made me quit." Christina rolled her eyes over at her mother. "But wow! Father went along with you! That floors me." She closed her eyes and shook her head. "And to think I always thought you two were so far apart.

"Shows how confused I was—just didn't get the dynamics between you two. For example . . ." She paused, then decided to continue. "Listen to this. In sixth grade our teacher asked us to write one paragraph describing our families. I described the two of you, the Reverend and Mrs. Ladd, as *the Ladders*—each so different, living like the outer edges of a ladder—two upright poles dug deeply into the ground—separated, connected only by a single rung which was me."

"Oh, Christina."

"Yeah. Shows how little I knew about how in love and together you two actually were."

"But you *did* see that we *both* were connected to you. And that was good."

"All I know is that I'm thankful, Mother. Thankful Father opened his heart to me so I could feel his love and my own for him before it was too late. His coming to me was a real miracle."

"The Lord at work is what I see." Ellen placed her napkin in her lap and leaned into Christina, her eyes misty.

"Mother, what is it?"

"There's a lot you don't know about your father that will floor you," Ellen smiled. "And now that he's gone there's something I need to tell you. Something he never wanted you to know—at least while he was alive."

"My God, Mother—oops, sorry, what?"

"It's a hard story. Not one a mother would ordinarily share about herself. But, now it's time for me to tell you."

Ellen leaned forward, her fingers wrapped in a ball on the table. She moistened her lips and blinked as though she had something in her eye.

Christina wondered, what's this about?

"After college in 1957," Ellen started, "I moved away from my parents' farm to teach in Silver Spring, Maryland where I met Robert. He was the assistant pastor at the church I attended, an earnest young man drawn to me I guess because I was so different—adventuresome, even frivolous. And before long we became lovers."

"You slept with Father before you were married?" Christina could scarcely believe what she was hearing. Especially that her father . . . "Wow!"

"Yes, I did. And there's more. Several months later, I fell hard for a tall, handsome blonde pilot training at the Naval Academy. I dropped Robert and started to sleep with Harold."

This story gets better and better, Christina thought.

"I was just a flitting around young girl having a ball. Your father only found out about all of that when Harold was killed in a flight training exhibition and I told Robert I was pregnant."

"Oh, my God!"

"Christina, please."

"Sorry Mother. It's hard to take in what you're saying."

"Imagine how Robert felt. I was pregnant with another man's child. But Robert never hesitated. He proposed immediately and we were married back home in my parents' church."

"So I'm . . . I'm not Father's daughter?"

"Of course you are. He raised you—shaped who you are today."

"But this Harold is my bio dad?"

"Biologically, yes. But Robert was and always will be your true father."

"But . . ."

"No buts. Your father stepped right in—never once mentioned Harold after he proposed. Never once."

"But don't you think all of that affected the way he treated me?"

"No, I don't. And you shouldn't either. I've told you how his parents were—old-world disciplinarians. They were his only models for parenting."

"You're right, Mother. I have to keep remembering that." She paused. "So Harold had blonde hair?"

"Yes. What about it?"

"Because Sammy's golden curls always surprised us."

"Well, now you know."

Christina stopped. Her head was spinning but she knew she shouldn't question any further. It'd been a load for her mother to get through. "Thank you, Mother, for telling me all of this. It couldn't have been easy for you. After I digest it all, can we talk some more?"

"Of course, Christina. Just remember—your father loved you very much. And I know he cherished having you as his daughter. You keep remembering that." Ellen looked down and pulled a photo from her purse. "This is for you. I knew the day would come when you'd want to see what Harold looked like."

"A lot like Sammy! I always thought Sam favored me, but look at this guy! Same oval face and blonde curls—just like Sam's. Thankfully, I saved one lovely curl from Sam's first haircut. Am keeping it in a blue heart-shaped porcelain box. And now I have a picture of his bio grandfather. Thank you Mother for saving it for me."

"Just remember, Christina, Harold was a wonderful man but Robert was your true father and I don't want you to ever forget that."

What a story, Christina thought. And I'm a little surprised about mother. In the fifties getting pregnant was every girl's nightmare. But no, she shook her head. As I go over it again, the more I can actually imagine Mother, back then not yet the tranquil woman she's become, but a high-spirited, light-stepping girl swinging along in her pleated skirt and angora sweater, circle pin on her shoulder, full of herself, enjoying sex, letting possible consequences slip from her mind.

But Father! Wow! It's hard—almost impossible—for

me to picture him as a lover casually enjoying premarital sex. Shows how little I knew, or even contemplated about my parents.

The next day Christina asked Penny to have lunch at Banjo's rather than in Renewal's luncheonette so she could share her mother's amazing story. Banjo's had been their favorite dive since high school. Christina still loved its funkiness—its low-brow décor and always booming rock music.

Have a Coke plastic circles were taped on all the walls and in-between were plastic bags containing stuffed animals placed high enough so little hands couldn't grab them.

Christina smiled at the two young girls all dolled up in black tees and red baseball caps, the red and black banjo on each bill bobbing as they giggled, simultaneously taking her order and sneaking eager eyes at a tall kid getting ice from the Coke machine.

"Did you see that top Lou was wearing today?"

"Yeah. Way too retro. Thank you, Ma'am, here's your receipt."

Oh my God, Christina thought. I guess to them I am a *ma'am*. Slipping into a booth with her diet Coke, she turned her wrist to look at her watch. Typical Penny. Late as usual.

She smiled at a grandpa sitting two tables over. His belly bulged over the belt of his pants as he laughed at his little grandson swirling a wet straw, drops squirting onto his bifocals. Christina liked his energy. I bet he's a grandpa with good stories to tell, she thought.

But another elderly man sitting over in a corner booth, coughing and spitting into his grayish handkerchief, chilled her as he stroked the arm of a pre-school girl. His greedy-eye energy made Christina wonder what his smile concealed.

"Sorry I'm late," Penny huffed as she plopped into a chair. "Did you order our burgers?"

"Did." Christina signaled the girls that they were ready.

After they had squirted ketchup on their burgers and fries, Christina began to tell Penny her mother's story. And she was surprised to feel an unexpected twinge of anger.

"Babe, I see some anger. What's with that?" You're the one who always talks about things not being what they seem. So what's going on?"

"I guess I feel cheated—not knowing who my father actually was while I was growing up. Maybe if I'd known all this stuff I would've better understood how Father treated me."

"Hold it right there. What you *do* know is that he respected you and cared for you. Your mother's right. He was a trustworthy father."

"Yes but . . ."

"Yes, but what?"

"I always wished I'd had a father who would hold me on his lap, kiss me, tell me how much he loved me. I always envied the girls who bragged about being able to wrap their dads around their little fingers. Doesn't every girl deserve a little of that?"

"Who knows what anyone deserves? I bet some of the mothers of those daddy girls sometimes feel pre-empted by their husbands' attachment to their daughters. In any case Babe, you need to keep things in perspective. Your father's goodness *is* a big deal. It means he didn't have his dick inside you from the time you were eleven."

Christina stared at her friend. "Oh my God! You always told me you were badly abused but not this detail."

"How could I tell you such a God-awful thing when we were kids? I felt so filthy I wouldn't even have known how to get the words out. My father was a monster, a pig. There was no slow initiation. He completely raped me the first time. Tore up my little girl insides. It's probably why I've never once gotten pregnant."

"Oh Pen . . ."

"There are so many gross details burned inside of me. It was ugly. He always kept his left hand over my mouth while he was doing it, then pushed my face way up and sloppily kissed me when he was done. Grotesque.

"But what happened after a while was even more grotesque. You're the only one I'd ever tell this to, Christina.

"My father found after a few months that he could turn me on. Touch me in just the right way and I would orgasm. Couldn't help it—he was so persistent. I began to crave the release, ignoring his salacious smirk while he was doing it. It felt good. Now how sick is that?"

"No Pen, no. You . . ."

"Stop! It was plenty sick to enjoy my own father doing me. Today I understand he was sicker. But not back then. I was eleven, twelve, a baby. He finally stopped when I got my period. But he had stolen all my little girlness. I was never the same.

"I was filled with shame because I still craved the release and that's when I became promiscuous, letting any boy who wanted to, have me."

"Oh my God! You know Pen, back then, even with all the hippie sex filling the air, I was so not clued in— was completely retarded in that department. I had no idea about that side of your life."

"Because I worked hard to keep it a secret from you.

And I felt lucky you never picked up on any of the boys bragging."

"But I thought we told each other *everything*."

"Not that, Sunday School Girl. I didn't want to lose you."

"That never would've happened."

"Well, I worried. You were an anchor for me."

"Oh Penny . . ."

"Yeah, that father stuff completely fucked me up and fucked up all my relationships 'til I met Lance.

"God, where was your mother?"

"Nursing her bottle. When I finally confronted her as I was trying to get my act together before college she actually fell apart. Claimed she never knew. But I don't believe that. Not for one minute. I think it was why she was always drinking. That's a pretty good clue."

"My God, Pen. I'm speechless. What you were going through while I was arguing with Father about whether or not I could listen to *Jesus Christ, Superstar*. You're remarkable!"

"Yeah well, Babe, we each have our own path in life. As the Buddha says, it's all about how we walk that path."

Penny dipped a fry into catsup, took a bite, and leaned sideways into Christina. "Now don't flip out on me, but get ready Babe, I've got *big* news. There's a new person on my path!"

"*What*? *Who*?

"His name is Nick. I think I'm in love!"

"God. Here we go again. You're *in love* and I've never even heard there's a guy? Pissed again, Pen, pissed again."

"Come on, Babe. You know how I sometimes keep secrets until I'm sure about something."

"Is that supposed to make me feel better?

"Definitely. Especially when I tell you about him. I met him at that Buddhist retreat I went to. He's a life coach with an MSW just like me and he's fantastic!

"Pen, it's still weird. I see you or talk to you on the phone every day. Doesn't it strike you as even a little strange that you've never told me you're dating this guy, let alone being in love with him?"

"Well . . . Okay. Maybe a little."

"You need to look at this secrecy pattern. I guess it goes back to all you had to hold in as a young girl, but it could cause a problem especially in your new relationship. And I can tell you, it definitely hurts my feelings."

"Oh God, Babe. I'm so, so sorry. I *will* think about what you've said." She picked at her fries, then put down her fork. "So can I tell you about Nick now?"

"Couldn't stop you. Do you care for him as much as you cared for Lance?"

"Oh Babe. As you know, each person brings

something different to a relationship and I think it's true that you never fully get over your first deep love, you just move on. Lance saved me with his love and kindness. Back then I was unformed in so many ways and Lance guided me to the light. Now, with Nick, I'm a more mature person. So our relationship is about going forward together rather than looking back."

"Sounds wonderful."

"It is. And," she paused, "it's important to me that you get to know him and like him. Because he's the real thing."

"Wow! Wait 'til Sarah hears."

"I promise I'll tell both of you more next time we get together. Now quit being pissed." She stood up and pointed to a crumb on the side of Christina's mouth. "I know you love me no matter what—have known that forever. You're definitely my safe corner." She pulled out a twenty from her wallet and dropped it on the table. "For our lunch. But I have to fly back to Renewal. Lucky you—you have the afternoon with Zack."

"After I take a few minutes to assimilate all you've shared. God, Penny, you're totally amazing." Christina stood up and kissed Penny's cheek, then held her in a hug until Penny pushed away. "Enough already. See you tomorrow."

She felt disturbed by Penny's story. Everyone has a

shadow side, she thought, but Pen's dad was evil. I can say that with a clear conscience. She closed her eyes and began her deep breathing. Breathing in I feel thankful. Breathing out I send positive energy into the world. Well, thank God, she thought. Pen's met somebody. I hope he really is good enough for her. She sat quietly for a few moments and when she looked up she couldn't help smiling at the little girl who was walking to a table with her mother.

Although it was steaming outside, she was wearing a daffodil yellow coat with a lacy collar and a straw hat with pink and yellow ribbons and an elastic under her chin.

Christina chuckled to herself imagining the tug that must have gone on when the child had insisted on dressing like that in the sweltering heat.

But, looking at the child's mother, she changed her mind. The woman smiled down at the child as she led her by the hand. She was a heavy woman, maybe three hundred pounds, and was wearing a colorful, flowered tent dress with a scooped out neck. And at the nape of her neck was an exquisite deep purple hummingbird tattoo. Good for her, Christina thought, she's not afraid to show off her own unique beauty. I like her energy and I think she's the kind of mother who would be easy with a determined little girl. She definitely lifts my spirits.

But, as she was leaving Banjo's, her mood quickly shifted. Coming in was the stalk of a woman with her stringy daughter—the two Christina had seen at Friendly's a few weeks earlier. It was hard not to recognize them. As Christina held the door open for them the child stared up at her, her eyes behind the thick glasses as blank as ping-pong balls.

Oh my God, Christina thought. I wonder if that child's going through something similar to what Penny endured—but going through it with her mother. Makes me sick to think of it.

CHAPTER 19

Christina and Sarah were driving along, both thinking about their destination. Finally Christina said, "I can't believe Mrs. Milton called and asked you to pick up any of Sandra's clothes you might want for your girls. Pretty strange."

"Bizarre! And why on earth didn't she pack up all of the child's clothes and send them along with her in the first place?"

"Maybe Mr. Milton sneaked Sandra away when his wife was sleeping or out of the house. She did say he *stole* Sandra."

The women again continued along in silence unable to let go of thoughts about the little girl they had both grown fond of.

Eventually Sarah rolled down her window. "The sun

feels good," she said, "I love Connecticut. Its beauty's much different from Georgia's where I grew up. These winding roads framed by the stone walls are particularly picturesque."

"Yeah, they go back maybe two hundred years. They were formed by the tossed stones thrown to the side as farmers cleared their fields. Then, as the piles grew, they began to serve as property lines."

"That's a lot of stone."

"I read somewhere that at one time there were actually two hundred and forty thousand miles of these walls throughout the six New England states." Christina looked over at her friend and winked. "And think of all the secrets behind those walls."

They both laughed. Then Christina turned serious. "I've been thinking, Sarah. This isn't a secret—more of a dream. I've been thinking that after my divorce is finalized I'd like to start the process of adopting a little Chinese girl."

"I'm not surprised. Remember, I was there with you during the Laurel Rose disappointment."

"Part of my crazy time. What did I know? Look at the handsome, adorable, bright, perfect little boy I got. I wouldn't exchange Zachary for a million little girls. But now might be the time to adopt before he gets too old."

"From what I've read overseas adoptions can take two to three years, so if you're serious you should get going."

"One of my concerns is that, because of my age and maybe because I'm single, they'll want me to adopt an older child. And, I may be selfish, but I don't want to do that. I want one more chance to hold a freshly hatched baby in my arms."

"You know, don't you, that you won't get a newborn?"

"I do. But I mean I would like a baby still in infancy—as close to newly hatched as possible."

"It's a big step and an exciting one. Pray about it, Christina." Sarah turned on her blinker and said, "It's right here around the corner."

Mrs. Milton led them down the second floor hallway and pushed open a door on the left. "This is Crystal's room. Take a peak."

"Crystal?" Sarah asked.

"My daughter who died—my little princess. She was only six. I haven't changed a thing in her room."

"I'm so sorry," Sarah said. What a terrible loss. The room is lovely."

The two women looked around at the pale pink room with its crisp white lacy curtains, snowy white bedspread embroidered with dancing fairies carrying lollypops and balloons, and the ballerina music box on a shiny white chest. But, when Sarah reached over to squeeze Mrs. Milton's hand, she pulled it away as if it was on fire.

"I know it's strange never to change a room—to keep cleaning it every week. I know it and I can imagine what you think. But, unless you've been through what I have, you can't understand."

Sarah nodded while Christina thought, I'd like to give you an earful about what both Sarah and I have been through.

"I've never gotten over it. This room has been my only consolation. Makes me feel she's still here—well almost, but not quite." Then, obviously forcing herself to move on, she closed the door and led the women to the hallway closet where Sandra's dresses, jeans and tees were hanging.

"Please take whatever you want for your girls," she said to Sarah. "I always bought Barbara the same quality clothing I bought Crystal at Lord and Taylor so I hate to give anything away to Goodwill."

Sarah nodded and sorted through the clothes. "If you're sure Sandra doesn't want you to send these to her I know my girls will feel happy to be sharing them."

"Please. Take all of them." She handed Sarah several large bags. "I won't be sending anything to Barbara."

Christina and Sarah were speechless as they drove away. Sarah finally said, "That poor, poor sick woman. Holding on to a dead child and rejecting a live one."

"Oh God. That house is bulging with sorrow. No wonder her husband took Sandra away. That's a broken woman who doesn't want to be fixed." Christina took a tissue from her purse and wiped the drip from her nose. "It's unbelievably sad. She even rejected Sandra's name. Insisted on an entirely different one. Now that's *really* strange."

"Yeah. Remember the afternoon Allene and Allison were giggling calling each other Ali-Pali? And Sandra asked if anyone else called them Ali-Pali? They told her nope—that it was their special name for each other?"

"I do remember. And I remember Sandra saying my daddy calls me Sandy Dandy or Dandy Sandy. Which sent all three girls giggling into a heap on the floor chanting Ali-Pali, Ali-Pali, Sandy Dandy, Dandy Sandy."

"You have another tissue?"

Christina dug back into her purse. "Here. You know, Sarah, I doubt that moving to Oregon even with a father who loves her will automatically remedy her dermatillomania."

"That's why I was relieved to learn from my friend, the school nurse, that notations about the picking were placed on the school records forwarded to her new school in Portland."

"Good. But, my God—that child has a lot to work through. Her heart is surely broken. What could be sadder than the heart of a child who could never find a safe corner with her own mother?"

The next morning Christina was relaxing in her favorite chair out on the patio, sipping her morning coffee, and enjoying the tweetings and buzzings as spring tiptoed in. But she couldn't get Sandra off her mind. Nature is so awesome, she thought, the seasons' differences predictable and on schedule. Wouldn't it be wonderful if humans were as predictable and reliable. And once more I keep wondering how a loving God fits into the equation.

Restless, she took a pair of gardening shears off the unbrella table and stepped down into her herbal garden to cut off some basil. Well, from what Sarah's told me, I know her pastor would say it wasn't God who arranged such a situation but Mrs. Milton's choice that arranged it—by her decision to have a child she wasn't prepared to love. I'm going to call Pastor for an appointment, see if talking with him will clarify things for me.

"I'm trying to come to grips with where I am spiritually so I can find the right path for myself," Christina explained to Pastor Armistead. "My divorce will soon be final and I want to be spiritually grounded for whatever decisions I must soon make." She felt relieved by the informal way the pastor sat across from her, one leg folded over the knee of the other, the sleeves of his striped shirt casually rolled up, his face friendly and open.

"Father was a minister," she continued, "so I got all the Christian teachings but I've pretty much come to question the basics. That began in a serious way after my first son was killed when for a long time I blamed God."

Pastor Armistead pulled his chair closer to hers. "Loss often presents one of faith's biggest challenges. Tell me more."

"Eventually my father led me past the blaming part by helping me understand that God doesn't intervene in the intrinsically impossible. But my faith has definitely been shaken.

"My close friend is a Buddhist and I've read the books she's lent me. While I'm intrigued with the Buddhist idea that there's no actual god out there but rather that the god nature resides in each of us, I can't quite go there."

"What part of your childhood faith is still important to you, Christina? I ask because you wouldn't be here if you weren't holding on to something."

"First let me say what I'm *not* holding on to. Because what I'm not holding on to is preventing me from ever again wanting to join a church. And that causes me concern because I have a son and so far I haven't a clue about how to spiritually guide him." She shifted uneasily in her chair, flicked off a loose thread from the front of her sweater.

"I no longer understand and maybe don't even accept the concept of the Trinity and I definitely can't accept the idea of the resurrection. Since believing all of that is what constitutes being a Christian, I have to accept that I'm no longer one of the flock. And that makes me uneasy because of my early background.

"But I do hold close in my heart the teachings of Jesus and I celebrate Christmas as a time of personal renewal symbolized in the birth of any infant."

"Christina, I can see that, although you're grappling with the details, you're interested in deepening as a spiritual being and that means you're on the right track."

"It's confusing because I *have* been comforted by the *Footprints* idea of Someone beyond myself carrying me through the hard times. Yet the concept of *Someone Out There* is hard for me to intellectually understand."

"Christina, that which is spiritual cannot be comprehended through your mind. It can only be understood through your heart.

"The truth is, Christina, people of faith all over the world are reaching for the path to God or Truth one way or another. The path chosen depends upon where each person is born and what each has been exposed to. You were reared a Christian and I see your struggle as the Holy Spirit working within you to bring you to your own spiritual truth whatever that may be.

"Here's a picture I was given years ago by one of the wisest persons I know." He spread out his arms and moved them into a semi-circle as though to embrace her as he spoke. "Visualize each seeking person as living on one spoke or another of an old-fashioned wagon wheel. The hub of that wheel is God or Truth. Each spoke represents a different belief system but all spokes lead to the God-Truth center. In the journey of faith, Christina, people are more alike than different."

Pastor Armistead leaned forward and took Christina's hand. "Go back and read the Buddha's teaching about the Noble Eightfold Path—Right View, Right Thinking, Right Speech, Right Action, Right Livelihood, Right Diligence, Right Mindfulness, and Right Concentration. Then re-read the Beatitudes in Matthew 5. You'll see the similarities. Although they come from different traditions, they're both guides to living a life of integrity.

"You're now at a crossroads and are concerned about making the right decisions for you and your son. I'm confident, because you're sincerely seeking the right path, that you will find it." He reached into a drawer and handed her a pamphlet. "Read this. We would welcome you to our upcoming *Life of Faith* series. It might help clarify things for you."

Well, Christina thought as she thanked the pastor and left his office, I like his inclusive attitude. And he was so kind to me and confident about my making the right choices. Maybe his study group could help me find my way. I'll have to follow the crumbs—see where they lead me.

CHAPTER 20

"Larry," Christina said, sitting across from him in a booth at Banjo's, "I'm totally devoted to my clients at Renewal and I don't feel I can leave them. Actually, I don't *want* to leave them. I'm sorry to disappoint you."

"I was hopeful at first, but when you didn't call back within a few days I realized nothing I'd said had lured you in."

"I love my work at Renewal too much to leave. But I've had several long talks with Basheera and I realize you have plenty of reason to be concerned."

"No kidding!" He stretched his legs out to the side of the table and leaned back in the booth. "These charter schools are publicly funded yet they hire only a few token female teachers. The majority hired are males culled from middle-Eastern countries. And their radical academic curriculum, though *advertised* as scientific, is totally inappropriate in a publicly funded school."

"How can they get away with it?" Christina waved to the young girl at the counter to bring more coffee.

"They also have deep private pockets and are able to fund their own publishing company which provides the books for their curriculum."

"What concerns me after talking with Basheera," Christina said, "is that her honor student daughter has been selected to participate in an overseas volunteer summer camp ostensibly to teach English to Muslim children. But she doesn't want to go because she's the only girl who's been recruited and she doesn't like the way she's being muscled around about it."

"I've told Basheera exactly what her daughter should do to get rejected from that program so I think I've resolved her worry there."

"Good."

"But," he grimaced, "our agency remains concerned about how the curriculum of Tabet and others like it is intended to immerse the most promising students into a radical Islamic culture founded on hatred of the United States."

"Makes me feel I'm deserting a valuable cause."

"Yeah." He winked at her. "You didn't take the hook."

"Come on, Larry . . ."

"Sorry. Couldn't resist pulling your leg a little."

"So how close is the agency to actually being able to challenge Tabet in court?"

"It's a long road because of the program's deep secretive roots. But we're betting on a new horse. We know that two distinguished reporters have been digging around for months and we're hoping for pay dirt. If they get it right, the public soon will get an earful about Tabet and that should put pressure on the courts in any ruling which comes before them."

He released his tightly laced fingers and leaned low across the table. "So Christina, where do we go from here?"

"We go nowhere. You're busy with Basheera and I may have met someone."

"Actually, Basheera and I have agreed to keep it at friendship." He reached across and took her hand. "So, if your new someone turns out to be not so great, how 'bout you and me?"

"Not sure I can walk down that road again."

"I'll call you next time I'm in."

Chapter 21

Penny's house party to honor all her friends and contacts who'd contributed to the fund she was managing to cover the costs of locating Dakota Callahan was swinging.

The minute Christina arrived Penny pulled her aside. "Babe, guess what?" Before Christina could answer Penny swung her around in a happy step. "The stick showed a plus and my ob-gyn agrees!"

"Oh my God! You're pregnant? I thought you said that would never happen."

"I *did* say that. But shows miracles *can* happen!"

"Pen, I'm thrilled for you! But one question. How long have you known?"

"Babe, you can't get pissed at me this time. I just saw my doc yesterday. Soon you'll see my little bump! Isn't that fantastic?"

"It really is! And God, Pen, I'm tickled to death for you. So where's Nick?"

"Couldn't come because he's running a seminar he didn't feel he could cancel."

"How's he doing with the news?"

"Blown away with a big head and puffed out chest. He also never expected it and at fifty he's more than ready."

"Any marriage plans?"

"Haven't gone there yet. The big thing is the baby. Really Babe, this is a dream come true for me. I can't even sleep I'm so excited."

"You better remedy that while you can because before you know it there'll be cries in the night."

"Don't care. I can't wait! But now I have to check the buffet. There's a surprise awaiting you. See you later."

Christina was immediately thinking baby clothes—blue or pink, this'll be fun. Penny'll be a great, unique mother. Definitely time to celebrate. I'm ready for a few drinks and a good time. Catching a glimpse of herself in one of the huge windows she felt confident about how slim she looked decked out in her new jeans and periwinkle halter top.

The sun, low in the horizon, glowed above the inlet casting a coral weave over the sand spread soft as flour along the shore. Further back the tall maples feathered out protectively around the dark firs offering shade to the clusters of guests gathered around the buffet.

Christina could hear the seagulls in the distance, could picture them swooping down for fish, and licked her lips thinking of Penny's delectable seafood spread. God, she thought, it's breathtaking here. And look how happy Zack is toddling after the children running around like madmen waving sparklers. "You're looking mighty alluring, Miss Christina."

"Chuck! My God! Who invited you?" Let me sink through the deck, she thought.

"Well Penny, of course. You must know your friend's not exactly bashful. Right after I met her at your house she called asking for a donation. Later sent me the invitation."

Just then a three year old crashed into Chuck's legs. He grinned and bent down, "Hi, little fellow. How 'bout I show you and your friends how to make balloon animals?"

Christina spun around looking for Penny.

"Don't dare say a word, because I won't believe you," Penny bubbled. "You should see your face—it's beaming like an electric bulb's been lit under your skin."

"I can't believe this. I told you I decided not to go on that bike ride with him."

"Yeah . . . So?"

"So why did you invite him without telling me"

"Wanted to. He's perfect for you—shut up and enjoy."

And off Penny went, her flaming ponytail swirling down the back of her hot pink tee, hips swaying in white shorts.

Christina had to admit as she watched Chuck playing so naturally with the children, twisting balloons into a dachshund, a rabbit, and a turtle, that she was intrigued. Actually, she was fizzing inside.

Later, during the fireworks, she didn't move when Chuck pushed in beside her, kicked off his sandals and swished his feet in the water, cozying close, as nuanced as a flashing light.

"Why wouldn't you go biking with me?"

"I told you. I'm just not ready."

"You sure look ready."

Christina blushed, aware of her halter clinging around her breasts.

"Well, I guess I'm in-between."

"In-between? Hm-m . . ." He slipped his arm around her shoulder striking up their overture—fever burning between them. Until Christina jumped up as the final splash of red, white, and blue burst in the sky.

"I've got to get home with Zachary."

"When can I see you? We're inevitable. You *know* that."

"Um—well, I guess Sarah would take care of Zack for me next Tuesday morning for a few hours."

"Can't you get away sooner?"

Her crotch was moist but, "No, not sooner."

"How early can I pick you up on Tuesday?"

"Eleven would be good." Oh my God, she thought. What am I doing?

Before she could change her mind, he pulled her close, brushed his lips lightly, tantalizingly across hers, his tongue barely touching her lower lip, "Eleven Tuesday it is." Then, with a wave to Penny, he was gone.

"Well Babe, looks like things are heating up."

"I can't even think—don't know what I'm doing. But I actually made a date with him."

"No surprise. Saw it about to happen all along. Face it, Babe, you're aching to wrap your legs around his neck."

That's precisely what Christina wanted to do. It was all she could think about driving home with Sarah, John and all their children.

CHAPTER 22

Sarah and her family were having dinner with Christina and Zack when Penny called, all excited, practically shouting over the speaker phone. "It's happened! Our investigator has found Allen! His name's Ashur Fontaine. And, listen to this—he's a graduate of a culinary school, studied pastry-making in Paris, and is now managing a restaurant his family owns in Atlanta. It's actually called *Ashur's*."

John couldn't stop grinning but the children watched wide-eyed as Sarah completely broke down. Christina hustled them into the family room, handed them a plate of oatmeal cookies, and slipped in *The Wizard of Oz* tape.

Penny was still on the phone telling John, "I've booked Sarah and Christina on Friday morning's early flight to Atlanta. I'll be waiting, dying to know what this Ashur's like."

Sarah cried into the phone, "Girl how will I ever repay you?"

"Meet your son. Get closure. That's enough for me. And call with a full report after you've met him."

"Definitely. Oh my goodness, Penny. This's a dream come true!"

Christina and Sarah were dizzy with delight—like school girls in their first-class seats—each ordering a bloody Mary before digging into crab salad on warm croissants, seasoned chips, and creamy cheese cake all resting on lacy paper-lined trays.

"I can't believe this is happening."

"Me either. The only thing bothering me is wondering if Brad will respect my wishes that he not bring his girlfriend into our house."

"You're sure you two can't work it out?"

"Out of the question. We did have that sweet moment the day of Father's funeral but, other than that, it's all gone. I can never forget how he betrayed me with the gate. Besides," she hesitated, glancing almost shyly at Sarah, "don't forget I have that date with Chuck on Tuesday."

Christina easily read Sarah's sigh, knowing it was about her rushing into things. She moved on. "We'll be getting into Atlanta around noon. Hopefully we can rest and take a dip before dinner. Penny made reservations for seven, so we should have plenty of time."

"It's hard keeping up with that girl."

"That's Pen. A spinning rocket—has always been that way."

That evening, walking into the restaurant, Sarah's hand shivered on Christina's arm, her eyes misty. She whispered, "Christina, this is so-o upscale!"

"Gorgeous!" Christina replied.

The color scheme was muted—the wallpaper a striped light silver and mauve, and the gray carpeting thick and cushy. Ultra modern slim stainless steel lamps cast a shadow over the white linen tablecloth on their table where they were seated in stylishly curved arm chairs covered in a textured mauve design.

"Oh my God, this dinner was delicious," Christina said an hour later, wiping her lips. "The prime rib was a perfect juicy light pink and have you ever tasted such yummy salad?"

"Never. I couldn't quite place what ingredient gave it such a scrumptious taste. But my favorite was the chocolate pecan pie."

Christina watched fascinated as Sarah smoothly asked their waiter to thank the chef for their fantastic meal, especially the pie. To her delight, all of Sarah's earlier anxiety was gone from her face. And she looked stunning in her navy suit and light magenta silk blouse, a strand of pearls at her neckline with silver and pearl drop earrings.

"You wanted to speak to me, Madame?"

It was Ashur! Six feet tall, broad shoulders, with a handsomely carved nut brown face above his starched chef's jacket.

"Yes, I wanted to tell you this is the best chocolate pecan pie I've ever had."

"We're happy to hear that, Madame. It's my grand-mother's family recipe. Actually, most of the items on our menu are either hers or my mother's."

"Well, everything was absolutely delicious," Christina added. "We're from out-of-town and are glad a friend recommended your place. We especially also enjoyed your salad. It was the one which tasted a bit like sesame and raspberry, but not exactly."

"That dressing's one of Mother's specialties. She's right over there. Why don't you tell her yourself?" He turned and motioned to an attractive woman about fifty talking at another table. "It's been our pleasure serving you, ladies. Stop in again while you're in town."

Sarah's eyes were bright as Mrs. Fontaine moved to their table. She was elegantly dressed in a high collared white silk tunic-style dress, a large gold pin with an emerald stone at her neckline. Her thick hair, clearly her glory, was swept up in a French twist with an orchid tucked in.

Again, as Christina watched with delight, Sarah's hand shot right out. "We loved your salad dressing—the one with raspberry."

"Why thank you. That does seem to be a favorite around here. We don't share our recipes but I'll give you a hint—its unique taste is due to a dib of sesame seed mixed with a dab of our imported sherry."

"A dib and a dab," Sarah nodded. "Guess I'll have to experiment when we get home."

"Where are you ladies from?"

Christina saw Sarah hesitate before answering, "Connecticut."

"New England's a beautiful part of the country. When our children were small we used to take them to Vermont skiing. Actually our son Ashur whom you just met loves to ski, but now he goes to either Vail or Aspen whenever he can pull himself away from our business." She paused and smiled broadly. "Thank you for all your kind words and come back to see us again sometime." Christina immediately piped up. "We'll be leaving Atlanta on Sunday but perhaps we'll come back for dinner tomorrow night because your food's incredible."

"If you like, I'll take your reservation now because

Saturday is our busiest night and I surely would like to accommodate you."

Sarah could barely contain herself as they left. "I can't believe him, Christina. He's gorgeous, totally handsome! Isn't he amazing? And his mother—gracious and casually amusing with the dib and dab. I can't believe I've finally met Allen—Ashur. Wait 'til I tell John! Wait 'til we tell Penny! And you! Fantastic, reserving for tomorrow! Even if I don't get to talk to Ashur again, I'll feel close just being in his restaurant. You can't imagine how blessed I feel to have finally met him. To see how he's turned out!"

"I'm almost as thrilled as you. And that smile on your shining face! It glows like a cut diamond!"

"Do you think there'll ever be a time when he'd want to meet me?"

"Sad to remind you, but he's already spoken to that issue. And truthfully, seeing the life he has here, I doubt if he'd risk upsetting things. He seems to have it made."

"You're right. I have to be satisfied. And thank the good Lord that He allowed me to find my son."

Christina wanted to say we should thank Pen's investigator, but zipped in the words.

The next evening Christina and Sarah were glad they'd made reservations as the dining room was packed and there was a huge wedding reception going on in one of the private rooms. They could hear the music and laughter and it was obvious the staff was stretched to the max. Nevertheless Ashur, dressed in a handsome gray stripped suit with a crisp white shirt and dark maroon tie, came right over to greet them.

"Welcome back. Returnees are always a good sign. Tonight we're featuring Lazy Man's Lobster. We do all the work for you in the kitchen so what you get are the tender chunks of lobster ready to be dipped in butter. We've learned our customers love not having to crack and dig to get to the good stuff."

"I'll definitely have that," said Sarah, beaming up at him.

The two women lingered a long time over their meal, Sarah feasting her eyes upon Ashur as he hosted guests to their tables. When Christina whispered, "Aren't you proud of him?" Sarah nodded, her eyes filling as they had off and on throughout their meal.

Christina smiled when Sarah excused herself to go to the restroom before they left. Then she jumped up and moved quickly to the wedding photographer who was taking pictures of the main dining room while he was waiting for the bride and groom to come out to their limo. When Christina saw him snap one of Ashur and his mother standing at the maître de stand, she handed him a fifty and her professional card and asked him to send her a copy of that picture.

"Madam, I can't do that. These photos belong to the

bride's mother. But with your fifty I can take a picture of you with them if you like and I'll send that to you."

"Better yet, here comes my friend. The Fontaines are still standing there. Please take one of my friend with them." And, before Sarah knew it, the picture was snapped and Asher and his mother were wishing them a safe trip home.

CHAPTER 23

The morning after their trip to Atlanta, Christina received an urgent call from Nick. Now she and Sarah, subdued and sad, were silently driving over to Penny's, news of Ashur way in the background.

They found Penny lying on a lounge chair on her deck, looking pale and fragile in a light green silk robe. Her glorious golden red hair straggled unwashed around her face.

Penny started to get up but her friends rushed over to her, pushed her back into her lounger and knelt at her side. Sobbing, Penny flung her arms around both of them. "How can it hurt so much to lose someone you've never known?"

"Oh but Pen, you *did* know your child," Christina said. "For two months you carried your baby inside of you, talked to him, thought about names. Of course you knew him. He or she was your dream come true—a vital part of you and Nick."

"I just can't seem to stop crying."

"And you won't for a while," Sarah said. "You've suffered a terrible loss—a little somebody you'd already bonded to. Why wouldn't your heart be broken?"

"It hurts so much," Penny sobbed. "I feel as though a chunk has been pulled out of me."

"You *have* lost an important chunk of yourself and you need to give yourself time to heal," Christina said.

"I have so much on my plate at work to take care of. But you know what? I don't give a damn. Right now I don't care about any of my responsibilities at Renewal. Don't care about a single woman we've been working with. Let Jackie act like an idiot staying with her brute of a husband. I just don't care."

"Pen, right now you don't have to care," Christina said, smoothing out the cuff on Penny's robe. "You have a great team who will fill in for you—women who themselves have suffered miscarriages or lost children in other ways. They'll know all about what you're going through and will want you to take care of yourself. You need to take time to grieve and let the rest of us do the heavy lifting."

"But I feel like such a baby. All I want is to be taken care of."

"Which is why we're here. Look what Sarah's brought over."

Reaching over to touch the bowl on the table, Penny quickly pulled her hand away but had already smelled Sarah's hot chicken soup. "It's not even eleven, but I'd love a bowl of that."

"Me too," Christina said, "because right now comfort food is what we all need."

Sarah came back from the kitchen with bowls and spoons. Before dishing out the soup she took Penny's hand. "This hurts so much right now, Penny. But, you know what? In another few months you and Nick can try again."

"But this baby was a miracle. I don't know if I'll ever be able to get pregnant again."

"Well, we'll pray for another miracle," Sarah said. "Now come on, let's chow down."

Sipping her soup and carefully watching her friend, Christina thought about how grief is the great equalizer. Yet we all experience it and handle it differently, she amended. Look how I raged, cried, brooded and begged why. And how Brad raged, drank, isolated and avoided. And if I know Penny—she's so used to denying her pain—she'll feel she needs to quickly pick herself up and move on. It'll take all I have to help her sit with herself and let the tears flow. But I'm determined to do exactly that.

She felt satisfied that the afternoon was a good beginning as the three women spent the entire time together eating and drinking, crying, comforting, napping in the sun until around five when Penny went in to take a shower while Christina and Sarah prepared dinner for her and Nick.

Penny seemed a little revived by her shower and looked beautiful in a new satin blush-colored robe, her curls moist around her face as, for the first time that day, she asked about Ashur and their trip to Atlanta. After she'd squeezed all the details out of them she fell back on her lounger and closed her eyes for a few quiet moments. When she opened them she assured her friends, "As the Buddha says, we all suffer in our lives. So I know my challenge—to gracefully walk this path and come out a stronger person."

"And I'm going to help you walk that path without your usual speed," Christina whispered as she pulled her oldest friend into a tight embrace.

CHAPTER 24

Christina fiddled around with her clothes on Monday evening. First one outfit—then another. She finally decided to go tailored—khaki shorts and a red tee with flat strappy sandals. It's been a long time since I've felt so excited, she admitted. How will I ever sleep?

"Anyone home?"

"My God, Chuck. I wasn't expecting you 'til eleven."

"Miss Christina, I couldn't wait one more minute." He pulled her into his arms brushing quick kisses all over her face. "Come on! Come on! I have a surprise for you."

Christina grabbed her purse, her other hand cozied in his, as they literally skipped to his truck, the rear bumper sticker boasting *Licensed Contractors Build Confidence*.

She felt hot thinking of the confidence part. And melted as he pulled her closer on the seat, his body steaming next to hers. After they'd parked in his driveway he excitedly drew her along. "You'll love this surprise," he said.

They walked about twenty-five yards across his groomed grassy yard and cut through a thick grove of trees. Christina gasped, "Oh my God, Chuck, this is gorgeous! A pond right on your property! It's beautiful!"

"Not as beautiful as you." And he pulled her down on a royal blue blanket, cushioning her head on a silky pillow. The rest was a melody between them, his passion pouring over her and into her smooth as baby oil as together they played their way into each other's secrets.

Afterward, Christina lay breathless, pressing herself closer and closer, tracing his cheekbones with one hand and drawing light circles in his ear with the other. She loved his muscled body and kept running her hand over his strong shoulders and hairy chest, so different from Brad's smooth one. For a moment the memory of Brad's chest came to her like a tear forming, but she shook it away as Chuck thrust into her again.

In between, they filled in some blanks. Chuck held her close, her head nested in his shoulder as he explained, "I started at the bottom working for a variety of companies during college vacations and for several years afterward before taking over Dad's company. Since his death I've been expanding like crazy and I love the challenge."

"What about your sisters? I feel envious you had so many because I was an only child. A lonely, only child."

He kissed her forehead. "That must've been hard." He kissed her again, brushed back her long tangled hair and pulled her still closer until there was only a dot of air between them. Then he added, "Well, my sisters are great—all interesting in different ways. With two older sisters and two younger ones, I was pretty spoiled. But I think having them made me a better man——made me more conscious of issues important to women."

"I like that," Christina murmured, nuzzling his neck. "How 'bout your mother? You said she died recently."

"Yeah, last year. That was hard for all of us."

"I know about loss." And then Christina told him about Sammy. When Chuck didn't just nod but asked her to tell him more about Sammy's specialness, Christina broke down and could go no further. He had touched where she lived.

Chuck whispered, "Let go, just let go," and smoothed her hair until she stopped crying. Then he asked, his finger twisting into one of her curls, "And when do I get to see more of Zack?"

"Oh Chuck. We need to go slowly with that. I don't

want to get his heart engaged until I know where this's going."

"Where do you want it to go?"

"Right now, if I could, I'd go to the moon with you. But just think. This is only the fourth time we've even seen each other. We need to get acquainted far better before I'll let Zack become involved."

"All I know is that I don't want this day to end. Don't want to take you home. Want to keep you right here tucked in my side."

"I love it here. But it's late—I promised Sarah I'd be back by two."

"When can I see you again?"

"Not easy. I've told you how busy I'm am with my work at Renewal. The rest of the time Zack needs the security of having me with him. So it's going to be difficult."

"We'll find a way." Chuck kissed her deeply, then brushed back her hair and ran his hand along her shoulders, pulling her tightly into his side as they walked back to his truck.

Christina floated with him in a swell of bliss.

CHAPTER 25

"Brad, what are you doing here on a Saturday morning?" Christina struggled to keep the annoyance in her voice in low gear. "You're supposed to call first."

"I know. But all we do is argue over the phone, so I thought I'd chance it and come on by."

"With an overnight bag?"

"Yeah. I have a meeting Monday in Springfield and I'm hoping you'll let me stay the weekend so I can have quality time with Zack." He smiled slightly. Enough to irk her.

"You've been impossible about my having him with me in the City. But the weekend I spent here with him while you were in Atlanta with Sarah was great." He put his bag down, put his hands in his pockets and leaned toward her. "So come on, Christina. Can I stay?"

She sighed. Blew out her cheeks, a frustrated frown on her face. "Okay. Come on in. He's just waking up. You can feed him. He'll love that. And put your bag in the guest room."

"Understood."

Well, Christina thought, at least Zack will have time with his daddy. He adores Brad and a weekend with him here at home will be fine as long as Brad stays out of my hair. In fact, this can be terrific. I can use the weekend to catch up without interruptions. Maybe even spend a first overnight with Chuck.

On Monday, because the weekend had gone so well, Christina softened and called Brad inviting him to stop by to have dinner with her and Zack rather than dining out on his way back to Manhattan.

"I've been thinking," she said, remembering all the times they'd sat together like this, sometimes happy, sometimes not, "maybe we should try this at least every other weekend. I like seeing you here with Zack and it certainly gives me time for myself."

"It could work at least in the short-term. But . . ."

Brad swallowed and put his fork down. "But, Christina, eventually you'll have to agree to let me have him weekends in New York."

"Sorry, Brad, but that will never happen until I meet your girlfriend."

"I haven't met *your* guy."

"True. But that's different."

"Different—how?"

"For one thing, I wasn't sneaking around with him when we were living together as a couple. And for another, I didn't even meet him until we were well into the divorce process."

"But still . . ."

"And I've come to know that Chuck has a fine character. Whereas I know nothing about the woman you're with—or even if you pick up different women at bars."

"Come on. You know that's not me."

"I don't know anything, Brad. Think of what I didn't know all those months you deceived me about the gate."

"So that's what this's all about. Pay-back time."

"No, Brad, I shouldn't have said that. I'm sorry." She dropped her forehead into her hand. "Just talk to me. It would be helpful for me to hear about the woman you're living with."

"I'm not exactly living with anyone right now. There was someone for a time, but that's over. But recently I've met a girl—a woman—who's pretty special."

He's finally saying it, Christina thought. "Well, good. I *want* you to be happy, Brad. We both deserve to move one. Tell me about her."

"Christina, that makes me too uncomfortable. Can we just let it go for now? If it develops into anything, I'll tell you."

Avoidant, as usual, she thought. And probably afraid—of what, I'm not sure. Probably that he'll tell me about this woman and then if it doesn't work out he'll be embarrassed.

"Just so you realize that it never works for us when you won't talk."

"Okay, okay. But anyway, thanks for the meal." He started to stand and then slipped back down. "Oh hell, Christina. I'm beat. Can I stay over one more night, get a good night's sleep, and drive into the City early tomorrow morning?"

"Fine. You can give Zack his bath and put him to bed."

In the middle of the night Zack threw up all over his crib. "Looks like my baby boy ate too much of his daddy's ice cream last night," Christina soothed, bathing him and tucking him back in.

The next morning she touched his forehead. No fever, but you still look pretty pale, Zachary-pachary. Good thing it's an at-home day for me. How 'bout watching Sesame Street for forty-five minutes while I make a casserole for dinner. Then Mommy will play with you.

Christina turned on the TV in the kitchen and started chopping onions and green peppers. Then looked up to see the plane barreling into the North Tower. She grabbed the clicker wildly switching from channel-to-channel, sure it was a hoax like the 1938 radio broadcast about the world being invaded by aliens.

But it wasn't a hoax. Smoke darkened the sky as the South Tower went down. Already they were saying that hundreds, probably thousands, of workers in the buildings had been killed. The tapes played over and over.

Beads of sweat trickled across Christina's forehead and into her armpits. She pushed the onions and peppers aside and fell into a chair. She knew that every Tuesday morning Brad met with an important group of clients in one of the towers. She couldn't remember which one. But now that didn't matter.

Sarah was there in minutes. "My God," Christina whispered, "how awful it will be for Zack to grow up without a father." They sipped coffee glued to the set, watching another plane crashing into the Pentagon and another into a field in Pennsylvania. They could see the sides of the buildings buckling, the fires flaring, the people holding hands and crying in disbelief. "Oh my

God," Christina cried. "Meredith and Miles! I'll have to go right over."

"Let's pray," Sarah said. She took Christina's hand and they bent their heads.

The morning ached along. Fortunately Zack had fallen asleep on the rug in front of the TV. Christina was dressing, trying to get up the courage to go over to Brad's parents and Sarah was making them grilled cheese when suddenly the phone shrieked through the kitchen. Christina pounced on it.

"Tia, it's me. I never got to the meeting."

"Oh my God, Brad! I can't believe it's you. I've been going crazy. You're really okay?"

"I couldn't get through any sooner. The lines have been jammed. But right now I'm in a bar with the exec I met early this morning for coffee. If we hadn't lingered over a third cup we would've been in the North."

"Nothing matters as long as you're safe. Oh my God, I was so scared."

"I know, Tia. But listen, please call my mom. Tell her I'm okay. Right now I'm spinning—not sure when I can get back in touch. But I have to stay here. See what I can learn about all of my business associates who were in one tower or the other." His voice quivered. "Besides, my new friend worked on the eighty-second floor of the North and I've got to find her."

Christina could hear his voice shaking. "Do what you have to, Brad. I'm just thankful you're alive. Call whenever you can. I'll call Meredith right away."

"So that's the way it is," she said to Sarah. "By the way he sounded, the friend must be his new sweetheart."

"At least Brad's alive. God works in mysterious ways."

"I wish I had your faith." Christina wasn't sure she should go on. But her thought was too powerful to ignore. "But Sarah, what about all the ones God didn't save?"

"That's part of the mystery. We can't know all of God's ways."

"But . . . For the fourth time that day Chuck was on the phone. "Chuck, Brad just called! He's okay. Never got to the North."

"Thank God. Can I come over? I want to be with you."

"Come."

Chapter 26

A few days later Penny grabbed Christina's arm as they came out of a group session. "Babe," she said, "school has started and you can see how many of our women here at Renewal are desperate for clothing for their kids, especially the little ones. Let's go to Target for the basics—jeans, tees, socks, sneaks, maybe some teddy bears."

"How 'bout the older kids?"

"Another day. They're harder to shop for and I haven't that much time. I have an appointment with the police chief at one-thirty to discuss where they are with the Dakota case. It's getting harder and harder for me to keep up my hopes."

"Okay, but there's my cell. Good it's Brad." She took a deep breath. "Brad, have you found your friend?"

"Not yet. It's impossible to find out about anyone. Looks like it'll be days, maybe weeks, but I have a hard time believing anyone working on the upper floors could've survived. What a nightmare!"

"When will you go back to work?"

"Don't know. Right now I have to pitch in. It's surreal here. Ash dropping everywhere, hard hats passing debris down the line in big buckets, everyone running on adrenaline. So I'm volunteering at a relief station handing out sandwiches, water, coffee to the exhausted rescue workers. I have to do it."

"It's the right thing. Just stay in touch." Christina turned to Penny. "I'm actually proud of him."

"Fine. But I don't think I'll ever star him on my calendar. Let's get going."

After they'd loaded their carts with basics for the kids, Penny insisted they head to cosmetics to troll for beauty. Christina smilingly followed her, happy to see her friend back to her normal bouncy self.

Penny held up a compact to Christina's face. "Babe, you're looking too pale. This is what you need—a rosier blush. And oh, look over here. What about a platinum rinse for me? Would add a little zip, right?"

"Pen, your hair's gorgeous. Leave it alone!"

"But I feel like experimenting. Look over here. It's the leg-tanning cream last Wednesday's paper said was the best deal on the market. Let's get some. Neutral for you, medium for me."

Christina took a tube, smiling and shaking her head, thinking what a girl, as they headed for check-out. "Wow," she said over her shoulder, "looks like everyone had the same idea about shopping for school." They parked at the back of a long line and, while Penny paged through *People*, Christina did her usual people-watching.

Standing right in front of them was a mother with her young daughter. They were dressed in identical red blouses and navy skirts, their hair parted in the middle clipped Dutch-boy style—short and straight—right below their ears. The mother must do the sewing, Christina thought, but God, they look like two over-ripe tomatoes. She watched as the girl played with the bracelets on her mother's wrist and her mother gave the child a little tickle under her chin. Well, Christina thought, they have their own special bond and I guess they think they look great. So what if they look too hot-house to me?

Then she turned to Penny. "Pen, this line is going to take forever. I'm going to the rest room. Be right back."

As Christina headed to the corner she noticed a woman walking out of the ladies' room fiddling with the fly of her pants. She recognized her as the stalk of a woman she'd seen at Friendly's and then at Banjo's with the unhappy little girl. As Christina's gaze fell upon the child's hands, soft and droopy, holding onto the handle of their cart, she saw the little strawberry on the girl's left hand. It was covered with makeup, but she could still see exactly what it was.

Oh my God! She rushed back to Penny. Pulled her away from their basket. "Pen, that woman over there is a man and the little girl is Dakota!"

"*What?*"

"Pen, I'm positive. The child has a strawberry on her left hand. Get the cops! Hurry! I won't let them out of my sight. We can't let them leave the store."

"God Babe, are you absolutely sure?"

"Positive. Hurry! I'll follow them."

It's bizarre I know, Christina thought as she followed the two into girls' wear. But as soon as I saw the birthmark on the child's hand, a picture flashed in my head of the many men I've seen coming out of restrooms checking their flies. *That's* something women don't do. They tug at both sides of their pants, pull down their tops, adjust their handbags on their shoulders, but they don't check their flies. Still, nothing might've registered if I hadn't seen the birthmark.

The *woman* was at check-out when the squad arrived. A female officer immediately checked the child's left hand and gently guided Dakota to the cruiser outside. His face was terrified as he turned once to see the *woman* being Mirandized.

She was actually Henry Stemp. As Christina and Penny stared at him they shuddered seeing his flat, greedy eyes. "They better nail his ass good," Penny said, "after what he's put that child through."

The news crews were all over what they called the *fly story*. Penny pushed Christina forward for the inevitable questions. Reporters came from all sides, microphones smack in her face. "How could you make such a quantum leap when you saw the woman checking her fly?"

"I probably wouldn't have paid any attention if I hadn't seen the birthmark on the child's hand. And I'd seen this woman twice before and didn't like her looks. Then something clicked in my head when I saw her checking her fly, remembering that that's what men do."

Customer's Eyes on Fly! Code Blue for Flies. Those were the headlines. It was a circus. The thrill of seeing the Callahans re-united rippled through the state as parents felt they could breathe easily once more.

But anyone watching Dakota in the pictures—huddled in his mother's arms, face blank, body rigid— quickly realized he still had both feet in the nightmare. Although Mr. Callahan tried to wave off the reporters it was impossible, The story went global, as the cameras kept zooming in on Dakota with Dylan clutching his legs.

When Stemp's face flashed on TV sans wig and makeup, Christina's lunch swelled in her throat seeing his defiant face, salaciousness gushing from his eyes— like filth from a sewer, she thought.

"What kind of person would put a child through that?" Sarah asked. "I can't even imagine it."

"Because you can't fathom evil," Penny answered. "The lead detective told us Stemp actually bragged about how easy it'd been to kidnap and hold Dakota," Penny continued.

"Stemp had been employed by the Department of Streets and Maintenance and was riding shotgun in the huge steamroller packing down the new macadam on the Callahans' street. On the morning of the kidnapping, Stemp called in his chips."

"His chips?" Sarah asked.

"Yeah. His partner, a Mario Paggati, had borrowed five thousand dollars to pay off gambling debts. Stemp told him to turn his eyes away and his debt would be cleared.

"So Paggati did exactly that. Looked away as Stemp reached down, grabbed Dakota, shoved a dirty rag into his mouth and pushed him to the floor. The steamroller sat so high above the road no one ever saw the child disappear. One minute he was playing ball on the sidewalk and the next he was gone."

"And that Paggati's another bad dude," Christina added. "He seemed oblivious to the enormity of what he'd done. Told the detectives, 'I needed an out. Wasn't my business if Stemp is a weirdo who likes little boys. Only thing I did was tell our boss Stemp had been called out of town and wouldn't be back to work.'"

A week later, Mrs. Callahan called Renewal for an appointment. Penny immediately told her she'd refer her to a trauma therapist, but Mrs. Callahan said both boys wanted to meet the *lady detectives*. "I'm not calling about therapy," she said.

Dylan was bursting with questions, wanting to know every detail about how Christina had recognized his brother, how she'd figured out the woman was a man, what he could do to become a detective when he grew up. But Dakota, hair cut and trimmed exactly like Dylan's, sat slumped over, body limp, eyes vacant. Penny took his hand and led both boys to the playroom so Christina could talk with Mrs. Callahan.

"Mrs. Callahan," Christina started, "Dakota's

suffering post-traumatic stress. He's lived through something no child should ever have to endure and we must take great care with him." She was disturbed to see Mrs. Callahan shaking her head, but continued anyway. "Dakota needs to see a trauma therapist immediately. In fact, your whole family has suffered an unspeakable ordeal and should be involved in that therapy."

"No, we don't want to do that. Dakota's so young my husband and I think we should do everything we can to help him forget what he's been through. We think talking to a therapist would stir up memories that shouldn't be disturbed—that talking about all of it would set him back even more. We want to put it all behind us as quickly as possible."

Christina almost jumped out of her chair. "But you can't get past it by *wishing* you could. You've already told me about his screaming nightmares and his insistence that the first floor windows be draped so the woman can't see him."

"Yes well, that's why we're planning a vacation, taking the boys to our timeshare in New Hampshire. This time of year the foliage should be beautiful. There's lots of room for them to run around and they love the mini-golf range and the indoor pool."

"But Mrs. Callahan I can assure you the feelings

Dakota's dealing with won't go away on their own. Believe me, a vacation won't help at all."

"But we believe it will."

"Unless he's helped to deal with his fright and confusion he's going to exhibit more and more desperate behavior—fear of almost everything, severe depression, and even suicidal thinking. And, if the later occurs, you'll never know what he might do when you're not around." Christina felt as though she was sinking in quicksand.

She tapped her hand in a loud snap on the table. "I don't want to scare you, but I've worked with the family of a ten year old who hung himself when his parents were grocery shopping. In his young mind he felt responsible for the death of his baby sister in an accident in which he had survived. No one had helped him work through those feelings and they ultimately overwhelmed him. That's why I urge you to get help for Dakota and for your entire family right now."

"We just aren't looking at it in that way. Everyone else keeps telling us to think positive—to get both boys involved in a lot of healthy activities."

"In such a severe case, Mrs. Callahan, distraction simply won't work. In fact, it'll be harmful."

"I know you're trying to be helpful," Mrs. Callahan said pushing back her chair, "but it's too much to keep going over. Thank you for all your kindness, but I agree with my husband—it was enough to live through and we'll be better off putting it behind us as quickly as possible."

With a leaden sigh, Christina handed her a large envelope. "Here's material on post-traumatic stress for you and your husband to read. You may feel differently after you've digested the facts. Please, please reconsider and let me made an appointment for you with a trauma therapist."

But I wouldn't place any bets on ever hearing from her again, Christina thought.

She returned home with a heavy heart. Usually she was able to put a boundary around her work at Renewal, to keep it separate from her life at home. But Dakota's plight chewed at her. Somehow, I can't let his situation rest. One way or another I'm going to check back with that family in another week or two. It *does* take a village and I'm not going to let that little boy down.

Oh God, and Jackie's another one, she thought. How can she stand constantly being beaten? I'm not going to let her down either. My best leverage is with her daughters who, thank God, continue to meet with me. Jackie's devoted to them and I'm hoping that in time her mother-love will kick in driving her to make the right decision about going to my house in Pennsylvania. She's got to do it. It's her only safe corner.

But will she? Christina sighed, poured a glass of chardonnay, and sank into her favorite lounger. What a day, she thought. It makes me wonder how long I want to stay at Renewal. A day like this makes me think more seriously about opening my own practice where people would pay for therapy and hopefully be more invested in changing their dysfunctional ways.

Then there's never-say-die Larry who actually dropped over the other day. Never called. Just dropped in—still working on me about Tabet. 'Just re-think it', he said. 'Basheera's daughter is now back in a public high school but she's been very clear that Tabet's program has a subversive aim and that the kids are being brainwashed by a velvet glove filled with steel. Strong words coming from such a young girl. So come on, Christina, give it a re-think. Since 9/11 everything's become more urgent.'

That hit hard, but I told him it's still no. Although within myself I'm wondering if I should give it more thought.

She placed her glass on the end table, slid her head onto the back rest and closed her eyes, hoping to stop her buzzing brain when she heard the mailman dropping mail through the slot in the front door.

When she saw the largest envelope in the bunch was

from Best Bridal Photography in Atlanta she tore it open, then speed dialed Sarah. "Sarah, come over. I've received a picture of you with Ashur and his mother and there's a letter enclosed from Mrs. Fontaine!"

Dear Mrs. Fletcher, they read.

> *A few months ago Ashur told me his birth mother from New England was looking for him.*
>
> *When I learned you and your friend were from Connecticut and, especially after you had the picture taken, I realized who your friend might be. I don't think I'm wrong but, if I am, please ignore what I have to say.*
>
> *Ashur will be getting married next spring and I think it's likely that when he and his wife decide to have a child he'll want to contact your friend for medical information. That's not a promise, but I know how careful and thorough my son is, which is why I think he'll do that. And I'll encourage him to do so.*
>
> *In the meantime, here's the picture, and please thank your friend for the precious gift of her son, my son Ashur.*
>
> *Sincerely,*
> *Beatrice Fontaine*

Sarah, tears rolling, jumped out of her chair. "Christina, this is everything I could've hoped for, could've dreamed of. What do you think?"

"With Mrs. Fontaine in the loop I feel pretty optimistic that one day you'll hear from your son. And that's fantastic!" She pulled Sarah into a hug and swirled her around in a happy dance.

"See Christina, it's what I always say—God works in mysterious ways.

CHAPTER 27

Christina sat quietly while Brad told her about Lily. "It's a miracle she's alive. They heard her cries under massive cement piles of debris. Unidentified, she was being cared for in the hospital in a coma all the time I was working in the volunteer tent.

"I had already returned to work when I got the shock of my life. Picked up the phone one morning and it was Lily."

"You genuinely care for her."

"Yes. And that's what I want to talk to you about."

"I'm listening." Christina reached over and patted his arm. "And I'm so sorry you had to go through all those weeks of pain and worry."

"Thanks, Tia."

She didn't fly off the handle when he used their Sammy name—just shook her head.

"Here's the thing . . ." Brad stood and paced for a few minutes, then sat back down. "Lily's in a bad physical and emotional state. She hasn't been able to return to work, sleeps little because of nightmares, and is like a pretzel stick from not eating. She desperately wants to get out of New York City."

"Understandable."

"But . . ." He began to pace all over again. "She wants to go back home to Seattle and wants me to go with her."

"And you're worried about Zack."

"Exactly."

"I can't help you with that. For myself, I could never leave our child."

"I knew you'd say something like that."

"What else would you expect me to say?"

"I know. I know. But Jesus . . ." He wet his lips and blew out his cheeks. "Christina, I feel I need a new start. And I love her."

Christina raised her eyebrows and shrugged her shoulders. "Again. What do you expect me to say?"

"Nothing, I guess. But what *do* I do about Zack?"

"Kiss away all his best little years." Christina felt a huge wave of sadness. Not because of Brad. But because of Zack. "What about your job?"

"I'll have to start all over. But, if I have to do it, Seattle's a good place to be. It's tech heaven."

"Sounds as though you've made up your mind."

"Close to it. But how will we arrange my visitations with Zack?"

"Until he's at least in second grade you'll have to come here to visit." She paused. "And, after that, you'll still have to come East to take him to Seattle because I'm *definitely* not putting him on a plane in the care of a flight attendant."

"It's about what I figured. You get to call all the shots."

"Right."

"It's not easy for me—having to start over. I loved the life we once had."

Oh God, thought Christina. Am I supposed to feel sorry for him?

"If I had it to do all over again I would've handled the gate differently."

"You don't need to go there."

"The way I handled that fucked everything up."

"It did. Not telling me immediately was a lie of omission oozing into our lives as indelibly as spilled ink." Christina sighed before going on. "But, you know Brad, I've found peace about the whole situation. And I've told you that. It's something I can't forget. But I *do* forgive you. So let's move on."

"Easier for you than for me."

"Probably. But more and more it's becoming clear

to me that life is nothing but a scale, always balancing gain and loss. We go along for a while with apples on the gain side, only a few peanuts on the loss side. Then in one swoop twenty pounds of peanuts are dumped down and the scale tilts to the loss side. We had a lot of good years, Brad. Years filled with rosy apples, the best of which were Sammy and Zack. Let's remember and be thankful for those."

"I'm so sorry, Christina. If I could do it all over again . . ."

Christina moved closer to him on the couch and gentled her hand along his shoulder. "I know. I'm sorry too."

Later, luxuriating in a warm bath, her neck resting on a rolled towel, her eyes closed, Christina paged through her happy years with Brad, the ones before Sammy died. They were good years, she thought. Nothing can take them away. He seems so broken right now I know it's up to me to be kinder to him.

She sighed as peace slid into her heart on soft slippers.

CHAPTER 28

"God Pen," Christina sighed as Penny flopped down on the sofa beside her, "once more I feel my life's taken a left turn. Brad's gone off to Seattle with Lily and now you tell me you're thinking of leaving Renewal to develop a program at the New Start Center in Manhattan."

"What a sad face! Look at you! You'd think I was going to Africa."

"Well, you've thrown me for a loop. I thought Renewal was your brainchild."

"My *first* brainchild, Babe." She smiled broadly up at Christina. "I love the new picture you framed for that wall. It's perfect over there."

"Don't change the subject." Christina leaned back and put her hand over her eyes. "Tell me *why*."

"Look," Penny thrust out a pleading hand, "I'm very proud of what we've accomplished here. But, reviewing this new offer, I realize how much my Renewal treatment model is one badly needed at New Start. Their program for women has not been anywhere near as successful as they'd hoped, their funding is in jeopardy, and their offer to me is very tempting—an important new challenge in a much larger setting."

"I know how impulsive you can be. Have you thought about the commute? Brad always found the train ride a drag."

"I'll get a rental near the office. Maybe spend a night or two with Nick. But don't worry, I'll always come back home on Friday evenings for the weekend."

"Just like Brad, you said you wanted to discuss this offer with me but I can tell you've already decided."

"Not true. Telling you about it right now is what's solidified it in my mind. So don't be pissed."

"Knowing you, I should've expected something like this. "So that's that." Christina took Penny's arm. "Come on out here. I've made the Pennsylvania Dutch molasses crumb pie you love so much."

Penny scooted up on the stool, grabbed a fork, and dug right in. "So-o, I've been thinking . . ."

"Dangerous."

"Would you consider joining me at New Start as the clinical director?"

"Absolutely not! Are you kidding? Mother gives me so much help here with Zack. It's the only way I can work at Renewal. Thanks, Pen, but New York's not for me right now or for a long, long time."

"I figured. But you're my first choice. So I had to ask. God Babe, this pie is fantastic. Maybe another piece?"

Christina pushed over the pie plate then clasped Penny's hand as she reached out. "Pen, I can't bear the thought of this. I missed you so much all those years you were in L.A. and now you're off again.

"Not the same, Babe. I'll be here Saturday and Sunday to hang with you and Zack. That is," she grinned, "if you two aren't over at Chuck's."

"As I've already told you, I'm trying to slow that down."

"And I think you're crazed. I really don't get it."

"He doesn't either. But he wants more of me than I'm ready to give."

"But things have been so hot between you two."

"I know. When we first met I was starved for comfort, for sex. My libido was driving me. But now that things have settled into normal I can better evaluate our situation."

"What situation, Babe? Chuck's a dream guy."

"It's hard to explain. For one thing, I'm not anywhere near ready to live with him which is what he wants. For another, I'm not certain he *is* the one. I was so sure from the beginning with Brad. Right now with Chuck it feels different. Maybe it's because of Zack—that I have to figure him into the mix. Or maybe I have second-chance jitters. I'm not sure what it is but I do know it's different than with Brad, and I need to slow it down."

"Just remember what I told you about Chuck being a gift to you from the Universe. I still think that."

"I haven't forgotten. And I *do* care for him a great deal. But I feel I need more time to be alone—just Zack and me. More time to run my life without being accountable to a partner."

"*That* can get pretty lonely, Babe."

"You forget I'm an only child—used to being alone. And remember, for five years after college I lived by myself when I worked for the agency in D.C. I liked it and I guess I want another go at that."

"Suit yourself. But, if you're smart, you'll keep the worm on the hook."

"I don't know . . . One of the things about Chuck that definitely bothers me is his heavy involvement with his church. Which he expects me to eventually join. When I told him I don't feel I will ever again want to participate in a mainstream church, he was hugely disappointed. So that could be a problem between us."

Penny looked down, a smile forming before she

asked, "Does that mean you're ready to join my Buddhist meditation group? I'll introduce you to everyone before I go. Think about it, Babe. You'd get a lot out of it."

"Maybe—at some point. I'm not sure I'm ready for that yet. I'm still sorting out what I really believe. Right now all I know is that I feel more centered—more like a spiritual person than a religious one. Which is why the idea of attending a church service turns me off."

"Sounds like progress to me." Penny shrugged her shoulders and walked into the den where Zachary was watching a tape.

She bent down and kissed his cheek. "Hi, darling boy. Got a kiss for Aunt Penny?" Barely taking his eyes off the TV he turned his head sideways and kissed her. "Love you Zackie."

Christina saw the mist in Penny's eyes when she returned to the kitchen and stood up to hug her. "Keep trying. You still have a few years left to try for that baby you want so badly."

"Oh Babe, I don't know if that'll ever happen. Nick and I have the opposite problem from you and Chuck. I'm ready to make it permanent but he's happy with the way things are. He feels that without a child there's no need to get married. Which is why I'm getting my own apartment. It'll do me absolutely no good to be a greedy-needy."

CHAPTER 29

"You sure you want to do this?" Chuck asked as he put the last suitcase in the trunk.

"Absolutely," Christina said, buckling Zack into his car seat. "I want to take these two weeks off from Renewal before Pen leaves permanently for Manhattan. And Grandma's house in Pennsylvania is the right place for peaceful reflection. Which is what I need right now."

"I'll miss you like crazy, that's all I can say."

"And I'll miss you. But I have to get going. Zack's about to fall off and the longer he sleeps the better." Christina put both arms around Chuck's neck and pulled him close. "I'll call tonight after we get settled."

A long kiss later she and Zack were on their way.

Christina's wings soared. Her heart sang, I'm on my

own, on my own! Free! Free at last! God, how good this feels, she thought. It's not as though anyone was actually holding me down. It was just a feeling I had—of being stuck.

She purposely drove leisurely, wanting to enjoy every minute. And broke into a chuckle when she spotted a dusty red Ford truck sporting the bumper sticker *If You Can't Run with the Big Dogs Stay on the Porch*. Immediately Brad popped into her mind. I guess that'll happen no matter how much time passes, she thought. At least we've gotten through the divorce. Thank God for that. She peaked in the rear view to see that Zachary was still out and slowly relaxed again into the drive.

Before long she found herself reminiscing about the bus trip she'd taken the summer of 1968 when she was eleven, traveling alone from Connecticut to Pennsylvania to spend the summer with her grandparents. It was a trip she'd frequently made with her mother so she'd felt confident and happy, even proud, traveling by herself.

And what an adventure it'd turned into! On the bus into the City she'd sat next to a tall guy with knee-hole jeans and a peace '68 sign stamped on his black tee. The entire trip he kept going over plans for the rally at some place called *the green* with the guy and girl in the opposite seats.

Christina remembered sitting there wide-eyed as they talked about the mace they were carrying for *the pigs*. She'd been too young and sheltered to know about the changes swirling around in the big world beyond her own as the three went on and on about white supremacy and male chauvinism. And she'd been totally amazed when her seat-mate—who'd ignored her the entire trip— took her hand as she stepped down at Port Authority. What a thrill that had been!

A thrill that had quickly vanished as she'd become mesmerized in the restroom by a woman with rolls of fat around her middle casually taking off her slacks and pulling on black mesh panty hose and silvery skin-tight shorts. Then had taken off her blouse and pushed it and the slacks into a large brown paper bag, bent over and plumped up her breasts into a sheer lacy black bra, slipped on a slinky gold strapless jersey, and strapped on spiked high heels. Christina chuckled remembering how, when the woman had given her the finger for staring, she'd torn out of the bathroom racing to find the lane for her next bus.

On that link she'd sat next to a woman about the same age as the other three. The woman sat crying, pushing one soaked tissue after another into an empty coffee cup braced in her lap, until finally Christina, overcoming her shyness, had asked what's wrong. 'My husband's been killed in Nam and I'm alone and pregnant.'

Speechless at first, Christina had finally drawn on the only words she could think of from home—'Well, I'm sure God has a plan for you.'

Christina winced remembering the woman's sharp bony elbow hitting her in the ribs as she spit out, 'Go to hell, little girl', and flew to a seat down behind the driver.

Well, she shrugged, I was just a child trying to do a good deed, to be a true girl scout. Funny how this drive brings so much back. It must be the smell of the Pennsylvania Dutch countryside—the scent of the alfalfa and the promise of the rich acres of corn. Somehow the Lehigh Valley always feels like home. And here we are!

Christina snuggled Zack against her shoulder and kissed his cheek, as she pushed open the door to the mudroom at the back entry leading into the kitchen. Grandma's pride and joys, a gleaming white electric stove and the top-bottom fridge still stood along the far wall facing the sink with its old-fashioned pump. I used to love pumping that thing, she remembered, helping Grandma wash the vegetables fresh from the garden.

As Zack scooted all over exploring, Christina dropped into the old rocker in the living room and looked around in satisfaction, happy that she'd kept Grandma's furnishings. It wouldn't be the same if I'd bought new things, she thought.

"Come on, Love Bug, let's see how you like your bed at Grandma's." The steeply pitched stairs led to a narrow hallway and three rooms—Grandpa's bedroom, Grandma's bedroom where her White treadle sewing machine still stood under one window, and a tiny bathroom they'd squeezed in from one end of Grandma's bedroom just a few years before both of her grandparents had died. 'Ach Cookie,' Grandma had said, 'going outside for our business got to be too much of a bodderation.'

Thank God for that, Christina thought, tucking Zack into a single day bed which stood a little apart from Grandma's double. "Now you're sleeping where I used to sleep," she whispered to Zack as she kissed his eyelids.

The days on the farm were as peaceful as Christina had hoped they would be. Zachary never tired of running around the wide green lawn, alternately playing with the toys from the large bag Christina had packed, pedalling his trike around the paved courtyard, or becoming fascinated with a new bug found in the grass or on some leaf.

Right now Christina chuckled as she watched him rolling down the hill on one side of the barn, running back to the top, throwing himself down, and rolling down over and over again. Just as I did as a child, she thought. What a blessing to see some of my life repeated in this beautiful, easy child. He was utterly adorable last night. We were lying on that hill on a blanket counting the stars when he asked me, 'Mommy, who cut a piece out of the moon?'

She was sprawled on the old hammock she'd dragged from the barn and scrubbed on their first full day before hanging it between two oaks. After one week in this beautiful setting, she thought, I've been better able to assimilate Pastor Armistead's words. Which is wonderful because they seem to have freed me of much of my God-anxiety.

In fact, the whole process I've been through since Sammy died, painful though it was, has left me feeling more grounded and solid. It's a good feeling. And I'm thankful now for a lot of my early teachings which I realize will guide me with Zachary. If I can show him by example how to live a loving, thoughtful life I will have accomplished what I should as his mother.

But right now I have this restless itch inside about my professional life. She inched herself out of the hammock and went over to the outside pump to fill a tin cup full of clear well water. I guess, to my surprise, I've gotten caught up in the whirl of changes all around me. She slid back into the hammock and rocked for a few minutes.

Pen wants me to develop a mental health program for the clients who've left their abusers but still come to Renewal for counseling. But, while I love working there, I'm not sure I want to stay much longer. And although private practice is looking more and more attractive to me I may want to spread my wings even further. Call it *the Larry effect*.

Now that he knows I'm definitely not interested in working at Tabet, he keeps calling me urging me to consider applying to the agency which is always looking for psychologists. And his repeatedly mentioning 9/11 is starting to get to me.

Working as an agent, perhaps under-cover, would be intriging—totally different from anything else I've ever done. The big issue there is that the agency has field offices all over the world and I wouldn't have a say about where I'd be assigned. So right now, before I go any further with that idea, I have to think about how I would deal with it if I were assigned, for example, to Butte, Montana or to Mexico City.

God, my heart is pounding, Christina thought. What's gotten into me? My life is fine as it is and yet here I go dreaming about making what would be a monumental change. I guess what draws me is not only the excitement but the feeling I'd be doing something constructive for our country—something that might make the world safer for Zackary.

Christina dropped one leg to the ground and pushed to re-start the hammock's sway. Then, she thought, there's still the idea of adopting. Am I ready and/or willing to give up the idea of Laurel Rose? I know Mother would like nothing better than having another grandbaby to help care for but, if I join the agency, would she want to pack up, leave her beautiful comfy home, and move to Berlin with me? My God, I have a lot of nerve even thinking of asking her to do that! I *definitely* need to chill.

She closed her eyes. Chuck's face drifted behind her lids. He loves me so much, Christina thought. Time. I need time. Breathing in, I will take in this moment. Breathing out, I will send out love. I am free. I can trust myself. I will cover myself with a blanket of calm.

Slowly Christina drifted into quiet and peaceful.

Until a sweaty little hand squeezed her arm. "Can we have popsicles for supper?"

"Popsicles? Nothing else?"

"Just popsicles, Mommy. The ones covered in chocolate."

"Hm-m. Popsicles covered in chocolate? Why not, Zachary-pachary. We're on vacation, aren't we?"

Christina pulled him giggling into her arms, blew raspberries into his sweaty neck and swung him around singing, "Zachary-pachary pudding pie, you smell so sweet oh come let's fly. Let's fly so high we reach the sky and never come back 'til next Fourth of July!"

CHAPTER 30

Christina and Sarah were sitting on the window seat in Christina's living room, looking out, waiting for Penny's car to appear. They were bundled up in silk long-johns and heavy sweats, their jackets, hats, and gloves on the chair opposite. It was still dark outside as they stared out letting their eyes adjust.

"I hope I'm not sorry I agreed to this," Sarah said, rubbing her hand along her cheek.

"Me too. But Pen has assured us that she knows Tim, the pilot, and that he has years of experience. She's been up with him twice already and swears we'll find it a hoot. At any rate, here she is. Grab your things."

"Look at the two of you! I told you to dress warmly, but are you expecting to go to the North Pole?"

"Well God, Pen. The sun isn't even up. It's *cold*."

"You'll soon forget all about that when we get there and you get caught up in the adventure." Christina and Sarah looked at each other, still skeptical.

But as they parked in the wide open field, the sun just rising, they felt themselves becoming excited as Penny pulled them over to where the crew was laying the hot air balloon for cold inflation.

"Oh my God, it's *huge*," Christina said giving Penny a shove. "You're sure it's safe?"

"Absolutely! Relax, Babe, you're going to love it."

"How long will we be up?"

"A little over an hour."

"Oh God. I hope it's as great as you say."

"You know I'm not crazy about heights, right?" asked Sarah.

"You told me. But relax. I swear you won't feel anything. The ride is super smooth and once we're up you'll be in so much awe you'll forget your fear." Penny took each of them by an arm and led them over to Tim who helped them board for their pre-flight orientation. Then they were aloft!

"Oh my goodness!" Sarah gave a thumbs up. "I don't even feel as though I'm all the way up here."

"That's because the hot air balloon floats with the wind so you never feel a blast against your face. Isn't it wonderful?"

"Pen, you were right. This *is* a real treat. It's totally awesome to see the beautiful Connecticut landscape from up here. And look! Over there you actually can see deer nibbling at the bushes!"

"So-o, my treat's a success?"

"Absolutely," said Sarah, giving another thumbs up. "I feel like a kid again."

"Me too. Only you would come up with this idea, Penny *Darling*!"

"Well, I wanted to do something special for my two best buds before I take off for Manhattan. Sure, I'll be back on weekends, but it'll be different from seeing you several times a week. But," she said, "let's not dwell on that now. Enjoy the view and get ready for champagne and a mimosa brunch when we land."

As Christina sipped her mimosa she marveled at the beauty and difference of her two friends. Penny, a tinkling bell always calling me to new things, she thought, making them shine in a different way. And Sarah, a delicate butterfly, spreading her wings around me and coaxing me to the light.

My life will change as I go along, she nodded to herself—probably in ways I never expected—but the friendship of these two women will always provide me and my darling son with a safe corner.